Deadly Close-up

". . . so don't freak out, I'm not going to do anything stupid," the voice was saying in a low, urgent tone. "But I should warn you, I usually get what I want."

Okay, that didn't sound so good. Vance had been on our suspect list all along. But what if he wasn't the culprit—but another victim? What if someone was in there threatening him right now?

Better safe than sorry. I tested the dressing room door. It was unlocked, so I quietly turned the knob and pushed.

The door swung open, revealing the interior of the trailer. I'd never been inside Vance's dressing room before. But I didn't have much time to take it in now.

Because all I could focus on was the long, deadly barrel of a gun.

Pointed straight at me.

THE HARDY BOYS

Undercover Brothers®

Available from Simon & Schuster

THE HARDY BOYS

Undercover Brothers®

BOYS

FRANKLIN W. DIXON

#38 Movie Mission

BOOK TWO IN THE DEATHSTALKER TRILOGY

Aladdin

New York   London   Toronto   Sydney

ALADDIN
An imprint of Simon & Schuster Children's Publishing Division
1230 Avenue of the Americas, New York, NY 10020
First Aladdin paperback edition September 2011
Copyright © 2011 by Simon & Schuster, Inc.
All rights reserved, including the right of reproduction in whole or in part in any form.
ALADDIN is a trademark of Simon & Schuster, Inc., and related logo is a registered trademark of Simon & Schuster, Inc.
THE HARDY BOYS MYSTERY STORIES is a trademark of
Simon & Schuster, Inc.
HARDY BOYS UNDERCOVER BROTHERS and related logo
are registered trademarks of Simon & Schuster, Inc.
For information about special discounts for bulk purchases,
please contact Simon & Schuster Special Sales at 1-866-506-1949
or business@simonandschuster.com.
The Simon & Schuster Speakers Bureau can bring authors to your live event.
For more information or to book an event, contact the
Simon & Schuster Speakers Bureau at 1-866-248-3049 or visit our website
at www.simonspeakers.com.
Designed by Karina Granda
The text of this book was set in Aldine 401 BT.
Manufactured in the United States of America 0811 OFF
10 9 8 7 6 5 4 3 2 1
Library of Congress Control Number 2010941302
ISBN 978-1-4424-0266-9
ISBN 978-1-4424-0267-6 (eBook)

TABLE OF CONTENTS

FRANK

1

Danger in the Dark

The city street was dark and deserted. The only sign of life was the pretty dark-haired girl hurrying along the sidewalk, huddled into her jacket.

Then she paused and looked back. What was that? Had she just heard footsteps behind her?

She listened for a second. Nothing.

Sucking in a nervous breath, she started moving again. When she reached the corner, she glanced both ways.

No traffic. No pedestrians. Nothing but the sleeping city behind her. The shadowy expanse of the park loomed on the far side of the street.

She scurried across and ducked into the park. Once again she stopped short, straining her ears.

This time she *knew* she'd heard footsteps. But when she looked back, there was no one there.

As she kept walking, she could feel someone watching her. She rushed down the twisting path, heading deeper into the park. She dashed from one streetlight's comforting glow to the next.

Footsteps crunched on the path behind her.

They were close. Way too close.

This time she didn't dare look back. She just walked faster, her breath coming in panicky gasps.

ZZT!

Suddenly the streetlight overhead blinked out, plunging the path into darkness. The girl let out a squeak of terror and scurried forward into the next puddle of light.

ZZT!

That light went dark too!

The girl froze, her eyes huge in the faint glow of the moon far overhead. A second later rough hands grabbed her, and someone clamped a hand over her mouth—

"Cut!"

A short man in his fifties with a neatly trimmed beard beamed at the girl as her "attacker" moved away. "Nice job, Anya." There was a smattering of applause from the onlookers huddled behind the movie cameras.

The girl smiled and shrugged off her jacket, which was way too heavy for the warm evening. "Thanks, Jaan. That was kind of fun."

Meanwhile I let out the breath I'd been holding. "Wow," I said to my brother, Joe. "That was a pretty cool scene."

"Yeah," Joe agreed. "Now I get why Jaan was so stubborn about filming it all in one long take. It definitely feels scarier and more intense."

I nodded, glancing around the location set. That was what the movie people called it, anyway.

It was really just a stretch of New York City ranging from Fifth Avenue to a few yards into Central Park. Some guards had roped it off from the public, and a handful of NYPD officers were standing outside to keep back gawkers.

Even so, there seemed to be at least as many people inside the ropes as outside them: the actress Anya Archer, director Jaan St. John, various production assistants, camera operators, sound techs, makeup artists, bodyguards, extras, and even the film's producer.

And, of course, Joe and me.

By now you're probably wondering what the two of us were doing inside those ropes. We're ATAC agents, not actors. ATAC—American Teens Against Crime—sends its teenage agents undercover to places where an adult agent would stand out like a polar bear at the equator. Places like a high school party. Or a skateboarding rally.

Or a movie set where most of the lead actors are under twenty years old.

This set fit the bill. The movie they were shooting was *Deathstalker*. It was based on the popular comic book series about an ordinary teenage girl who gets turned into a superhero when an alien spaceship crashes into her house and she's injected with a scorpion's poisonous venom.

Okay, so the story didn't make much sense to me. Then again, I stopped reading comic books when I was ten.

But Joe? He was totally geeked about it. With the emphasis on "geek."

Anyway, it was kind of cool getting to hang around the set. The Deathstalker movie was really big budget. There had even been a nationwide talent search for the perfect actress to play the title role.

That was how they'd found Anya. She'd never acted before the day her friends dragged her to the audition.

"Anya's doing great today," Joe said. "You'd never know she's not that experienced. It's hard to believe that someone wants her off this film so badly."

"Someone else besides Myles, you mean?"
I grimaced. "Yeah. But the cops are sure he's telling the truth about what he did and didn't do."

Myles was a Deathstalker superfan. We'd met him at a science fiction and comics convention in New Jersey. It turned out he hated that Anya was cast as Deathstalker and was trying to make trouble for her.

But we'd learned that he wasn't the only one.

"So he pulled most of the stunts at the convention," Joe went on. "But he didn't set the fires."

"Or rig that microphone to electrocute her," I added.

Joe nodded. "Or send most of the text messages. So who did?"

"If we knew that, we wouldn't still be here." I shot a look at Anya, who was talking to Jaan nearby. Who was trying to get rid of her?

We'd been called in to find out. And it wasn't turning out to be easy.

Aside from a few location shots like this one, most of the filming had taken place on a totally closed set with guards posted at the gates 24/7. Some of the incidents had even taken place *inside* those gates. For instance, someone left a creepy cut-up photo of Anya in her dressing room and then set her trailer on fire.

There was other stuff too. She'd received threatening text messages. Plus, a lot of scary stuff had happened at the convention. Like I said, Myles had confessed to some of it.

But not all of it. Which left us exactly where we'd started.

Nowhere.

I checked my watch. "It's been more than twenty-four hours since we got back from the convention," I said. "And we haven't found out anything useful all day."

"All we can do is keep working on it, bro," Joe said. "Talk to people, see what turns up."

Typical Joe response. He's a go-with-the-flow kind of guy.

Me? Well, Joe would probably call me an overachiever. Let's just say I don't like spinning my wheels and getting nowhere. And that was the feeling I was getting right now.

Just then I noticed a woman in her sixties with a tidy gray bun stepping toward us. Uh-oh, time to stop discussing the mission. Like I said, we were undercover. Only Jaan and Anya knew why we were really there.

"You must be so proud of Anya, Frank," the

older woman said, giving me a pat on the arm. "I can tell that was difficult for her, but she pushed through and did it. You'd better give her a big hug and kiss for that."

I did my best not to blush. See, that was part of our cover story. I was posing as Anya's boyfriend from back home in Minnesota. Joe was supposed to be my friend who'd landed a job as an extra on the film.

Let's just say he was a lot more comfortable with his role than I was with mine.

Joe would say that's because I'm hopeless with girls. Don't tell him, but he's sort of right. What can I say? I'll face down a crazed criminal with a gun any day of the week. But trying to come up with something witty and interesting to say to a cute girl? Now *that's* scary.

"Um, sure, I guess," I told the woman, Vivian Van Houten.

She was an agent for actors, though she wasn't Anya's. We hadn't even met Anya's agent, who'd been in L.A. since we'd arrived.

Vivian represented Harmony Caldwell, a popular young TV actress who was playing Deathstalker's best friend, Susie Q. Harmony had finished her scenes earlier in the day and left, but Vivian was still hanging around. I guess she wanted to be moral support for Anya. The grandmotherly woman seemed to have taken the inexperienced actress under her wing.

"Yeah, he's totally proud." Joe smirked slightly, then raised his voice. "Hey, Anya!" he called. "Come on over so your boyfriend can congratulate you on doing such a great job!"

Anya heard him and rushed over. "Thanks!" she exclaimed, flinging both arms around me.

Gulp. Okay, lung function zero. I told myself it was because she was squeezing me so tightly it was physically impossible for me to breathe properly.

Yeah, that had to be it.

"I really did it that time, didn't I?" Anya said happily, still squeezing. "It's all thanks to Jaan and Zolo—they've been helping me so much."

"Zolo?" Joe sounded a little surprised. Zolo Watson was another teen actor on the film. He was playing Asp, Deathstalker's alien sidekick. The role suited him. He was weird enough to be from outer space.

I knew why Joe was surprised. We didn't know Zolo and Anya were friends. Zolo mostly seemed to keep to himself.

But I wasn't really focused on that at the moment. I had my hands full—literally. Anya was still clinging to me, and I wasn't quite sure where to put my hands.

After a second she pulled back and smiled sheepishly. "Of course, it would have been nice if I got it on the first take instead of the . . ." She let her voice trail off. "How many was it, Anson?"

She glanced at a young man standing nearby. I hadn't really noticed him before. He had sandy-brown hair and an anxious expression on his freckled face. He was one of the production assistants, I guessed.

Anson checked his clipboard. "That was take twenty-six," he said.

"Don't remind me. I thought we'd be here all night."

I didn't have to look to tell who'd spoken this time. It was Stan Redmond, the producer of the film. When I glanced at him, his droopy jowls were practically quivering with impatience. The guy was pretty tightly wound. I couldn't blame him. Trying to keep a nutty creative genius type like Jaan St. John on any kind of schedule or budget had to be a challenge.

Anya's face fell. "Sorry, Stan," she said. "I was trying my best, I really was."

Stan's grumpy expression softened. A little.

"I'm not blaming you, Anya," he said. "*You're* not the one who insisted on filming that scene in one long take so that *each* time there was even the *smallest* mess-up, we had to start shooting from the very beginning." He glared at Jaan, who had just wandered over to join us.

Jaan seemed unperturbed. "Ah, but it shall all be worth it in the end," he said. "Now should we finish on a good note and call it a night? We can shoot Parker's panic scene tomorrow evening."

"No!" Stan barked out. "We're ten days behind schedule as it is. Besides, you can't just go shutting down a major Manhattan intersection anytime you please. That doesn't just happen, you know. If you're planning to shoot anything else here, you'd better get it done tonight."

I could see his point. Getting this setup wasn't easy. For this scene moviegoers needed to believe that Deathstalker was being followed along the deserted city streets late at night. The truth was a little different. It wasn't that late—maybe nine o'clock. And the streets were far from deserted. Just beyond the roped-off area, there was tons of traffic. Jaan had explained that the sound people would edit out the blaring taxi horns and squealing brakes.

And just outside the ropes, tons of people had gathered to watch the filming. Some were snapping photos with their cell phones. Others were just gawking.

"All right, if you insist, we'll keep going." Jaan shrugged. "But where is Vance?"

The nervous-looking PA, Anson, stepped forward. "I've been texting him his revised call time as we go along," he said. "He should've been here, like, fifteen minutes ago."

Stan rolled his eyes. "Actors!" he muttered. "Hang on, I'll call him." The producer pulled out his cell phone.

"Cool," Joe whispered to me. "Maybe we'll finally have a chance to talk to Vance. That dude's harder to pin down than a greased pig. But once we do, it won't be hard to get him to talk—about himself anyway."

Vance Bainbridge was another teen actor. He was also one of our suspects. We'd found out that he'd wanted his girlfriend, well-known actress Amy Alvaro, to play the role of Deathstalker.

Did he want that badly enough to try to scare Anya into quitting? We weren't sure yet. Partly because we hadn't been able to get him alone all day.

A moment later Stan hung up. "It's going straight to voice mail," he said with a frown.

"Then I suppose we'll have to alert him the old-fashioned way," Jaan said. "Anson, would you mind dashing back to the set and letting

Vance know we're ready for him now?"

The PA nodded, but before he could move, I stepped forward. "I'll go get Vance," I volunteered. "I mean, if it would be helpful."

"Thank you, my boy." Jaan smiled at me. "Indeed it would. That way Anson can help us get set up so that no time is wasted once Vance arrives." Shooting a quick look toward Stan, he added slyly, "And all of us can get back to our hotel rooms that much sooner to sleep off the stresses of today."

I didn't stick around to see if Stan responded to that. "Back soon," I murmured to Joe as I passed him. "See if you can talk to a few more people while I'm gone."

"I'm on it, bro."

The main movie set was in another part of the park. When I got there, the guards at the gate recognized me and nodded me through. I headed for the row of trailers where the primary actors had their dressing rooms. Most of the trailers were dark and quiet. Other than Anya and Vance, the main actors were all done for the night.

But a light was on in Vance's trailer. Good. I knocked on the door and waited. No answer.

Figuring he might be napping or something, I knocked again, but louder this time.

Again, nothing.

"Maybe he's listening to music," I said to myself.

Leaning forward, I pressed my ear against the door and listened. I didn't hear any music. But I did hear something—a low voice, talking fast.

Was it Vance? I couldn't tell.

I pressed harder, wishing I had some kind of high-tech ATAC gadget to help me hear through walls. But no such luck. Good thing my hearing's pretty good.

". . . so don't freak out, I'm not going to do anything stupid," the voice was saying in a low, urgent tone. "But I should warn you, I usually get what I want."

Okay, that didn't sound so good. Vance had been on our suspect list all along. But what if he wasn't the culprit—but another victim? What if someone was in there threatening him right now?

Better safe than sorry. I tested the dressing room door. It was unlocked, so I quietly turned the knob and pushed.

The door swung open, revealing the interior of the trailer. I'd never been inside Vance's dressing room before. But I didn't have much time to take it in now.

Because all I could focus on was the long, deadly barrel of a gun.

Pointed straight at me.

Crowd Control

It's not easy being related to the world's dorkiest dork.

Okay, maybe that's an exaggeration. A little.

But seriously, only Frank would find an excuse to split when he had a gorgeous girl like Anya hanging all over him.

Yeah, I know what he'd say. It was the perfect opportunity to catch Vance alone for a few minutes. But dude, come on! If I was the one playing Anya's boyfriend? I'd so be sending *him* off instead.

But hey, that's me. I'm not allergic to girls like Frank is.

Anyway, Anya didn't seem to take it personally. "So what's new?" she asked me quietly as Frank took off like a tall, nerdy jackrabbit. "Have you guys made any progress today?"

"Not much," I admitted, glancing around. "But don't worry, we're working on it."

That reminded me. I was supposed to talk to people. But who? Nobody around me was really a suspect.

Well, except for Jaan. For one crazy moment at the convention, we'd thought he might be behind the trouble. He was one of the only people who had full access to the set. And to Anya.

Also, he had lied to us. Frank and I had seen him arguing with a man at the convention. When we'd asked him about it, he'd pretended not to know what we were talking about.

But we were over that now. For one thing, we'd figured out that the man was probably just Anya's old bodyguard, Big Bobby. What we'd witnessed was Jaan firing him for always being late. No biggie.

Besides, he was the one who brought us in. Why would the director call in ATAC if he was the bad guy? Even Jaan wasn't that crazy. Was he?

A couple of extras were standing nearby. I noticed one of them staring at me. He was a teenage guy with a big nose and glasses.

"Dude," he said to me. "Are you in the next scene, or what?"

"Um, huh?" I said, too distracted to pay much attention. "I mean no, I don't think so."

The guy traded a look with his friend. "Okay," the second extra said. "So then what are you doing here? You weren't in the last scene either."

"Bro, what are you, my agent or something?" I grinned weakly. "Uh, I'm just here to watch."

Anya stepped a little closer. "Frank and I invited him to come watch tonight's scenes," she told the extras. "Joe's very interested in learning all about acting. He wants to observe as much as he can."

"Hmm . . ." The first guy looked skeptical. "For someone who's supposed to be so interested in acting, you sure don't seem to do much of it."

"Yeah," his friend added. "Have you even been in a scene since you got here?"

"I only got here yesterday morning," I pointed out. "I'm just, you know, taking it slow."

Just then one of the makeup artists hurried over. "Ready for your touch-ups?" she asked the extras. "We'll be getting started soon, and Jaan wants you guys to be ready."

The extras wandered off after her, leaving me and Anya in relative privacy again.

"Thanks," I told her. "Guess my cover isn't quite as tight as I thought."

"Don't worry about them," she said. "So you

and Frank don't have any new ideas about who's behind all the trouble? I mean, I really hoped when you caught that guy at the convention that it would all be over."

"We did too," I agreed. "But we'll figure it out. We're still talking to people, trying to narrow down the—"

I was cut off by an excited voice calling Anya's name. Glancing over, I saw a couple of college-age guys in Deathstalker T-shirts right outside the roped-off area. They were pushing at the bodyguards, trying to get closer.

Anya smiled and waved. But her smile looked kind of forced.

"Can we get out of here?" she murmured to me.

I looked around. There wasn't much privacy on the location set. We were like zoo animals—safely separated from the crowd, but totally on display.

Anya's new bodyguard was standing nearby. Big dude with a skull earring and a fade. His huge muscles made him almost as wide as he was tall. And he was pretty tall.

"We could hide behind Moose," I joked.

She actually cracked a real smile at that. But she still looked tense.

"This is the part I'm having trouble getting used to," she said. "All the attention. You know?"

"Yeah." I tried to imagine how it would feel being famous. Having people worship and adore you. Getting attention everywhere you went.

Okay, it mostly sounded pretty cool to me.

But I didn't say that. Part of our job was to make Anya feel safe. We had to protect her while we figured out who was trying to scare her. I tried to think of something comforting.

"Listen," I said. "I'm sure it gets easier. Being famous, I mean. At least that's what Vance, Harmony, and Vivian all say, right?"

She didn't respond. That was because she wasn't listening to me. She was staring at something past my left shoulder.

"What?" I said, turning to look. "Are you okay?"

She tuned back in to me. For a second she didn't answer.

Then she shrugged. "It's nothing," she said. "I just, um, thought I saw someone I knew out there."

"Really? Who?" I glanced that way again.

She bit her lip. "Big Bobby."

"Your old bodyguard?" This time I spun around for a better look. I scanned the crowd but didn't see any familiar faces.

"He's gone," Anya said. "Actually, I'm not even sure it was him. Probably not. Why would he hang around here after Jaan fired him?"

"Good question," I said. "Maybe I should—"

Once again, I didn't get to finish. There was a commotion at the other end of the set. Frank and Vance had arrived.

"Hey, Anya!" Vance shouted with a big grin on his face. "Think your boyfriend needs a hug—I just scared the daylights out of him."

"Huh?" I said, hurrying over with Anya right behind me. "What happened?"

By now everyone else was gathering around too. Frank didn't look nearly as amused as Vance.

"It was nothing," Frank said. "Vance and I just sort of, um, startled each other."

Vance smirked. "Yeah, you could say that."

Then he told the story. He'd been on the phone in his trailer and hadn't heard Frank knocking. When the door opened, he spun around, clutching the prop he was holding.

That prop? A nasty-looking shotgun. It had ended up pointing straight at Frank.

"Good thing it wasn't loaded, huh?" Vance said. "But sorry if I scared you, buddy. Here's a little something to make you feel better."

Reaching into his pocket, he pulled out something and tossed it in Frank's direction. Frank caught it one-handed.

"Nice reflexes," I told him.

Frank glanced at the item he'd just caught. "It's a key chain," he said, sounding confused.

"All right, no harm done, children," Jaan put in soothingly. "Now come—we won't need the gun prop in this particular scene. However, Vance will need hair and makeup. . . ."

He bustled Vance off toward the makeup artists. Meanwhile Stan stepped toward Frank and me. He glanced at the key chain in Frank's hand and frowned.

"Ugh, keep those things out of my sight," he grumbled.

I grabbed the key chain. It was made of metal and shaped like the Deathstalker logo—a golden scorpion. It had sharp little pincers and everything.

"What do you mean?" I asked Stan. "This thing's awesome!"

Stan looked annoyed. "It better be for as much as it cost!" he complained. "A certain someone"—he paused just long enough to shoot a disgruntled glance in Jaan's direction, though the director was well out of earshot—"insisted on special ordering them to hand out to fans at that convention,"

"Like swag, huh?" I said. "That's cool."

Stan frowned. "Maybe it would have been," he said. "Maybe the key chains would've drummed up enough interest in the film to make up for the outlandish cost of manufacturing them. Except for one thing. They didn't arrive on set until this morning! Twenty boxes of them, to be exact."

I winced. "Bummer," I said. "Still, I'm sure you can give them out some other time. Any fan would love to have one. That's good publicity, right?"

"Now you sound like Jaan," Stan told me. Judging from the cranky look on his face, that *wasn't* a compliment.

Just then someone called to him from across the set, and he hurried off. I pocketed the key chain and glanced at Frank.

"So did you get in any quality time with Vance between gunshots?" I asked.

He grimaced. "Take a guess. He spent the whole time ragging me about the gun thing."

I could believe it. It was tempting to pile on and do a little teasing myself. But we didn't have time for that right now. Not if we wanted to solve our mission.

"Something weird happened right before you got back," I said. "Anya thought she spotted Big Bobby watching the filming."

"Really?" Frank glanced toward the onlookers behind the ropes. "Did it look like the guy we saw yelling at Jaan yesterday?"

"Don't know. I didn't see him. By the time she

tried to point him out, he was lost in the crowd."

"Was she sure it was him?"

"Not really," I said. "But if it was, maybe we've got ourselves another suspect. He could be the one we've been after all along."

"How do you figure?"

"Think about it. Why would a guy who just got fired come hang around his old workplace?"

"Lots of reasons," Frank countered. "Maybe he was there looking for Jaan—trying to get him to hire him back, or just picking up his last paycheck, or whatever. Or he could be friends with the other bodyguards working the set today and have plans to meet them for dinner. Or—"

"Okay, okay," I broke in. "I hear you, and it's totally possible any of those things might be true—if it even *was* Big Bobby to start with." I watched idly as the makeup people finished with Vance and he headed over to Jaan. "But what if this is the clue we've been waiting for? Maybe Big Bobby has been behind the trouble all along."

"But why?"

"Who knows? Maybe scaring Anya could've been his warped way of getting some job security as her bodyguard."

"Hmm." Frank didn't look convinced.

But I was starting to like my new theory. Sure,

the motive was a little wacked. But who expects criminals to be logical? The rest of it made sense.

"He had access to Anya and her trailer," I went on, "so he totally could've done the stuff on set. We already know he was at the convention, too. And anyone with the cash to buy one of those disposable cell phones could've sent those untraceable texts."

Frank still looked a little skeptical, but nodded. "Worth checking into, I guess," he said. "Let's ask Anya to tell us more about him."

It was a while before we got a chance to talk to her. She was playing the happy little film student, sticking close by Jaan and watching as Vance shot his scene. That scene was pretty boring, if you ask me—just Vance racing up and down the street over and over again looking scared, while the cameras filmed him from every possible angle. But Anya seemed fascinated.

Finally Jaan was satisfied with the footage. "That's a wrap, my lovelies," he said. "The limos should be waiting to spirit you back to the hotel for some beauty rest."

We all headed for the cars. The bodyguards went first, moving the ropes to keep the crowd back. Frank and I caught up with Anya, who was walking with Vivian and Stan.

"Listen," I said to her in a low voice. "Can we talk to you for a second? We might have—"

"Anya! Over here, sweetheart!" a woman called from nearby in a strong New York accent.

Glancing over, I saw an older woman waving from the crowd of spectators. She was clutching a single red rose, holding it toward Anya.

"Whoa," I whispered to Frank. "For a second I thought that was Aunt Trudy. Scary!"

Frank grinned. Our father's sister has lived with us for years. She's family, and we love her. But she can be a little hard to take sometimes. Besides, I could only imagine what she'd say if she spotted us here. She's clueless about ATAC—she thought Frank and I were in Washington, D.C., right now at a Young Diplomats Conference. So did our mom. Dad's the only one who knows about ATAC, mostly because he started the agency.

Anyway, this woman looked a lot like Aunt Trudy. Same age, same gray hair, and sensible shoes and cardigan sweater. Same bossy tone to her voice, too.

"This is for you, Anya!" Not Aunt Trudy called. "A handsome young man asked me to give it to you. Too shy to do it himself, I suppose. Isn't that sweet?"

"A man? What man?" barked out Anya's bodyguard, Moose.

The woman cocked an eyebrow at him. "Is that any way to speak to your elders, young man?" she complained. "I swear, I don't know what this world is coming to sometimes!"

"Sorry, ma'am," Moose rumbled. "Just need to be careful."

I knew how he felt. Still, this woman didn't exactly seem like a prime suspect for any trouble. Well, not the criminal type of trouble, anyway. More like the interrupting-your-favorite-video-game-to-make-you-load-the-dishwasher type of trouble.

"Careful of what? Of a nice boy giving a flower to a pretty girl?" The woman glared at Moose. "Harrumph!"

"Yeah," I whispered to Frank. "I think she's definitely Aunt Trudy's long-lost twin!"

"It's okay, Moose. I'm sure she doesn't mean any harm." Anya stepped forward, looking kind of uncomfortable, and took the rose.

"There. Was that such a big fat hairy deal?" The woman shot Moose one last disgruntled look, then smiled at Anya. "I hope it works out, dear. You two would make such a lovely couple!"

"Um, thanks." Anya briefly returned her smile. Then she turned away, stepping toward the limos a few yards ahead.

Frank and I caught up to her again.

"Listen," Frank said. "We wanted to ask you about something."

Anya didn't respond. She was opening the little white card attached to the rose's stem. As she scanned it, her face froze.

"What?" I asked, immediately on alert. "Who's it from?"

She just shook her head. Then she dashed forward, jumped into one of the waiting limos, and slammed the door.

"Wait!" Frank called.

But it was too late. The car was already pulling out into traffic.

A moment later she was gone.

Moving Right Along

We arrived at the set bright and early the next morning. Well, what was left of it.

"Whoa," Joe said as we arrived. "What's going on?"

It was a good question. Half the trailers were gone. There were boxes and cartons sitting around everywhere. People were running around even more frantically than usual.

"Let's go find out," I said.

We hurried past the guards at the gate, who waved us through as usual. One of the first people we saw inside was a teen actor named Buzz Byers. He was watching several burly crew members maneuver a heavy rolling camera toward a waiting truck.

"Dude, what's happening?" Joe asked him. "Why are they dismantling the set?"

"You don't know? We're moving," Buzz replied.

"Moving?" I echoed.

Buzz nodded. "We're done at this location, at least for now. We're setting up down near the Empire State Building next." He shrugged and smiled. "Don't ask me for the details. I'm used to scenery changes, but nothing like this!"

Joe and I chuckled. Buzz was a successful Broadway actor who was making his first movie.

"Um, have you seen Anya?" I asked.

"Yeah, I think she's over at the craft services table." Buzz pointed.

Joe and I headed that way. "If she tries to run away when we ask about that flower note, tackle her," I said, only half joking.

"I hear you, bro." Joe rolled his eyes. "I never knew a pretty girl who had such bad luck with flowers."

"Yeah. First that bouquet at the con, and now this." I thought back to the flowers Anya had received during a panel discussion at the convention. That time, there'd been a nasty note tucked inside.

"But we already know Myles was behind that one. So who sent her a nastygram this time?" Joe wondered.

"And why did she run off like that when she read it?" I added. "If it was another threat or something, why wouldn't she tell us about it?"

"Only one person can answer that," Joe said. "And there she is."

Anya was picking at a platter of bagels. There was an anxious little crease in her forehead.

"Morning," I greeted her. "Listen, we need to ask you about what happened last night."

"Yeah," Joe added. "Specifically that flower. The note really seemed to freak you out."

"Oh." Anya wasn't really looking at us. She was staring across the way at a group of workers dismantling some scaffolding. "Uh, it was no big deal. Just a fan note, that's all."

"Really?" I said. "It looked like more than that to us."

Joe picked up a bagel and took a bite. "Like maybe another clue to this case," he said with his mouth full.

"Sorry about that." Anya shot us a quick look. "I was just tired, and I kind of overreacted. I guess notes in flowers just make me nervous now. . . ." She let her voice trail off, looking uncomfortable.

"We just want to make sure we've got all the info. Otherwise there's no way we'll be able to figure out who's after you. You have to let us know right away if anything suspicious happens, okay?" said Joe.

Anya nodded. She was watching the scaffolding guys again. Her blue eyes were troubled.

"This is weird," she said. "I just got used to being here on this set, and now we're moving." She sounded nervous and was shivering. I traded a look with Joe. We needed to work fast.

"Listen," I said. "Joe told me you saw Big Bobby in the crowd last night."

"I thought I did," Anya said. "It might've been someone else."

"Really?" Joe sounded skeptical. He waved his half-eaten bagel. "Isn't Big Bobby, like, seven feet tall with bright red hair? Seems like he'd be hard to miss."

"He's only six four," Anya corrected. "Anyway, like I said, I didn't get a good look. It was dark, and I was tired."

Joe started to say something else. But I nudged him to shut him up. Several people were heading toward us.

In the lead was Harmony Caldwell, the pretty blond actress who was playing Susie Q, Deathstalker's best friend. Behind her were her agent, Vivian, and a couple of extras.

"There you are, Anya!" Harmony called with a

smile. "Jaan asked me to grab you and bring you to the makeup tent. He wants to shoot a few close-ups of us while the set's coming down."

"Okay." Anya glanced at Joe and me. "See you guys later."

As she headed off with the others, Joe and I wandered in the opposite direction. "So the rose thing was a bust," Joe said, shoving the rest of his bagel in his mouth. "What next?"

I was already thinking through our suspect list. That was easy, since it was pretty short. "We still need to talk to Vance," I said. "Zolo, too."

Yeah, Zolo was on our list. We'd found out that in addition to acting, he was writing a screenplay. And he showed he had a fiery temper when others talked about it.

"What if he's counting on his role as Asp to get people interested in his script?" I said. "He'd want to do everything he can to guarantee that this film is a success."

"And maybe he thinks that's more likely if there's a big-name actress in the lead role instead of an unknown like Anya," Joe finished. "Even if that's not his motive, Zolo's such a freak show. It's not hard to imagine him causing trouble."

"Yeah," I said. "Anybody else still on the list?"

"What about Big Bobby?" Joe said. "If that

really was him that Anya saw last night . . ."

"Then he still doesn't have a strong motive," I finished. "Unless we go along with your theory about job security."

Before Joe could reply, we saw someone scurrying toward us. It was Anson, the skinny little PA we'd seen last night. He was clutching a clipboard, as usual. And he looked like he was about to have a nervous breakdown, as usual. At least as far as I could tell.

"Are you doing anything right now?" he blurted out, staring anxiously into my face. "Because I really need someone to help me—I'm supposed to get someone to throw out some boxes, and the guys who were supposed to do it disappeared, and—"

"Chill, bro," Joe broke in. "Just tell us what you need us to do and we're there."

Anson blinked a few times and glanced over at him. "Oh," he said. "Okay, thanks. Um, come with me."

He rushed off. Joe and I followed him to another part of the set. There was a line of big Dumpsters. Sitting near them were several sealed cardboard boxes.

"These are the ones we need someone to dump in the bins," Anson said, gesturing at the boxes.

"Uh, Anya said you're pretty strong, Frank. Maybe you could toss that one in a Dumpster?" He pointed to the largest box, which had weird symbols handwritten all over it, plus several big, blank stickers on the sides and top.

I felt my face turn red. Had Anya really told this random PA that I was strong? Why would she say something like that?

"Um, okay," I mumbled, looking over at Joe. I was sure Anson's comment was going to earn me some more ribbing.

But Joe wasn't paying any attention to me. A pair of cute teenage girls had just wandered into view. So of course, he was checking them out. Totally predictable.

"Good, thanks," Anson said. He pointed to the largest box again. "Just make sure this one gets dropped into a Dumpster. Okay, Frank?" Then he rushed off, disappearing behind a large camera crane standing nearby.

Joe was finally tuning in to what was happening. "Did I just hear that dude call you strong? Ha!" he boasted loudly, flexing his biceps and glancing at the pretty girls. "No way. I'd better take the heavy one, bro. Step aside."

"Be my guest," I said, grabbing one of the smaller boxes instead. It was light enough to toss up and over the eight-foot-high wall of the nearest Dumpster.

Joe hoisted the larger box, grunting dramatically. The pretty girls were watching.

"Are you with the set crew?" one of them asked Joe. "I thought you were an extra."

"No way, he's not an extra," her friend said. "If he was, we would've been in a scene with him by now, right?"

"I'm totally an extra," Joe said. "I'm, uh, new. That's probably why we haven't worked together yet. Anyway, I'm just helping out. You know, lending a little extra muscle."

He turned sideways, obviously trying to give them a better view of his muscles as he held the box. I rolled my eyes. We really didn't have time for this.

"Hurry up," I told him. "Let's get this stuff tossed out and get back to work."

He shot me an annoyed look. But he turned and headed to the Dumpster.

As he scaled the little metal ladder on the side, he grunted with effort. This time I was pretty sure he wasn't faking. The box looked pretty heavy. It was definitely way too heavy to toss over the side of the Dumpster like I'd done with the smaller one.

I was about to climb up and help him when I heard a shout. Glancing over my shoulder, I saw a man with wild dark hair standing behind me. He looked familiar, though I couldn't remember who he was at first.

Then I noticed that his hands looked black and kind of sooty, and it came to me. Jaan had pointed him out to us when we'd first arrived on set. His name was Scorch; he was the head special effects guy on the film. Jaan had called him a genius.

Scorch was staring at Joe, who'd just reached the top of the ladder. "What are you doing with that?" he cried. "Freeze!"

Joe paused just as he was about to drop the box. "Huh?" he said.

I stepped toward Scorch. "It's okay," I told him. "One of the PAs asked us to help out by tossing these boxes."

Scorch didn't answer. He pushed past me, running toward the Dumpster.

"Whatever you do, do NOT drop that box!" he shouted at Joe with an edge of terror in his voice. "It's full of live explosives!"

Scorched

I froze in place on the little metal ladder. "What?" I cried.

My muscles clenched as I clutched the box. Staring down at it, I noticed for the first time that some of the symbols scrawled on it looked like little flames. Uh-oh.

The special effects dude was sprinting toward the Dumpster. "Stay where you are!" he shouted. "I'm coming."

Yeah. Where exactly was he expecting me to go? I didn't bother to ask. All my focus was on not letting the box slip out of my grip.

It wasn't easy. The thing was heavy. I carefully pulled it back toward me a little. Just enough to rest one corner on the edge of the Dumpster.

That helped. But only a little. If I so much as sneezed, that box was going down.

I glanced into the Dumpster. It was almost empty. Nothing to soften the heavy box's fall before it hit the metal floor.

And blew me to bits.

I could feel sweat beading on my forehead. My muscles screamed in agony as I did my best to hold on. The SPFX guy—what was his name again?—was running toward me, but he seemed to be moving in slow motion.

Options raced through my head double time. What should I do? If I let the box fall, I was toast. I looked at the SPFX dude again. He'd finally reached the Dumpster and was scrambling up the ladder like a monkey.

"Hold still," he said breathlessly. "My name is Scorch. I'm going to try to get up next to you. We can work together to get the box back down."

I squeezed over as far as I could on the little ladder. The guy jostled me, and I felt my fingers slip a little.

"Careful, dude," I said. Okay, maybe it was more like *squeaked*.

"Easy," Scorch said. "Just let me grab the other corner. . . ."

He reached for the box. I felt it slip again. "Hold on!" I cried. "I'm losing my grip!"

"I've got it," Scorch said. "Climb down and I'll deal with this."

"No!" The dude was pretty skinny, not to mention a good thirty years older than me. No way was he going to be able to hang on all by himself. Plus, it was much harder to carry the box and climb down the ladder than it was to go up. "Like you said, we should work together to get it back to the ground."

"No. It's too dangerous!"

"So is this thing really packed with explosives?" I asked.

"Do I sound like I'm joking?" He didn't. "Who told you to touch this box, anyway? It's clearly marked to be moved by my crew only!"

"It is?" I glanced at the box. "I don't see anything like that."

Scorch looked down too. He frowned. "Someone put stickers over my warning labels!" he exclaimed. "But who—"

"Dude, this really isn't the time." I could feel the box slipping again. My hands were sweating now too. That didn't help. "Let's get it safe on the ground, and then figure it out. Okay?"

"What's going on up there?" Frank called up to us.

"We're coming down," I called back. "Clear

everyone away from here—at least, uh, twenty feet back."

"Make it forty," Scorch put in grimly.

"Got it. Be careful!" Frank hurried off. A few seconds later I could hear him ordering those cute extras to move away.

"Okay," I said to Scorch. "Here's a plan. Maybe we can slide it back over the edge, then you sort of hold it up from below and climb down slowly, while I support some of the weight from up here. Think that'll work?"

"Maybe." Scorch didn't sound too sure.

I wasn't too sure either. It would be better if I was underneath holding up the box. But it would be too hard to switch positions on that tiny ladder. We were going to have to make do.

"Good. Let's go," I said. I hoisted myself up on the edge of the Dumpster to get in a better position.

From here I looked into the next Dumpster, which was only a few feet away. Too bad we weren't dealing with that one. It was filled almost to the top with paper, broken-down cardboard boxes, packing peanuts, and stuff like that.

But whatever. We had to deal with what we had.

"Move down a step," I told Scorch, "and I'll—"

I didn't get to finish. Scorch was already taking a step down.

Or trying to, at least. His foot slipped on the lower rung, and he almost fell off the ladder.

"Aaah!" he cried, catching himself just in time.

As he did, his elbow hit the corner of the box.

"Noooo!" I yelled, trying to hold on.

But it was no good. The box was too heavy. And gravity wasn't on my side.

I watched hopelessly as it flew out of my grip.

"Joe!" Frank shouted, sounding really far away.

I barely heard him. I was acting on pure instinct now. Pushing off from the ladder, I flung myself away—over the gap and into that next Dumpster.

"Oof!" I grunted as the paper and boxes broke my fall.

KA-BLAAAAAAAAM!

The world seemed to explode around me. I dove deeper into the trash as chunks of debris rained down. A thick black wave of smoke rolled in and choked me.

A couple of pieces of paper in my Dumpster had caught on fire. I clambered to my feet, coughing and half-blind, and stomped them out as best I could.

My ears were ringing. Those metal walls caused a serious echo.

When the ringing faded, I heard screaming and shouting from outside. I kicked a few bits of garbage against one wall, then used the pile to get high enough to reach the top. My arms were kind of shaky. It took three tries to boost myself up.

It was chaos outside. Smoke was everywhere. The next Dumpster was a smoking wreck. People were running and screaming.

Except for Scorch. He was lying motionless on the ground below. Frank was checking his vitals. He glanced up when I called his name.

"Joe!" he exclaimed, sounding both relieved and worried. "You okay?"

"I'll live," I said. "How about him?"

"He's still with us," Frank said grimly. "But I have a feeling he's not going to be playing with fire again for a long time."

It was a good half hour before Frank and I got a chance to talk. First we had to put out the fire from the explosion. Then we had to wait for the ambulance, which somebody had called as soon as the box blew. When the medics got a look at me, they tried to load me into the ambulance along with Scorch. By then the nurse from the set's medical tent was there too, and I convinced them she could check me out instead.

Of course, then she insisted on actually doing so. I was stuck in the med tent for another fifteen minutes while she poked and prodded, seeming amazed that nothing was broken. She'd also sent someone to wardrobe to find me some clothes, since mine were kind of charred. The only things I was able to salvage were my wallet, my phone, and that Deathstalker key chain.

Finally the nurse let me go. I found Frank waiting outside, looking impatient.

"I've been asking around," he said. "Everyone says Scorch is super careful. Until now, he's never had an accident with explosives."

"Thanks for the concern, bro," I joked. "I'm fine, by the way."

He looked kind of sheepish. "Sorry. Glad you're okay. But we need to work fast and figure this out. I'm pretty sure this was no accident."

"No duh," I said. "But why would someone try to blow *us* up? Do you think our cover's blown?"

Frank looked troubled. "We thought Zolo might've overheard us talking about the mission that time at the convention. Maybe we were right."

"Maybe." I stopped short and turned to face him as another thought occurred to me. "But maybe *we* weren't the target. Maybe it was just *you*— because you're *Anya's boyfriend.*"

"Huh?"

"Think about it, bro," I said. "Anson specifically asked *you* to grab that box full of explosives. Then he took off like his pants were on fire before you could do it."

"So you think Anson wants me dead?" Frank sounded dubious. "Why? I barely know the guy."

I shrugged. "Who knows? Maybe he's got the hots for Anya and thinks if he gets rid of her boyfriend, he'll have a shot. Anyway, I think we'd better go talk to him."

We found Anson in the editing tent. When I touched him on the shoulder to get his attention, he almost jumped out of his skin.

Yeah, the guy was stressed. But was that all? Or was he surprised to see us both alive?

"I heard about the accident!" he blurted out before we could say a word. "Oh gosh, I'm so, so, so sorry! I don't even know what to say. I'm sure it's all my fault; I must have mistaken what Scorch, Jaan, and the others told me about which boxes were supposed to get trashed. It's just so hard to keep track sometimes when everyone's telling you what to do! Anyway, I'm just glad it turned out all right. Well, for everyone except Scorch." His face fell. "I heard he's going to need skin grafts."

"It's okay," I broke in. "But listen, do you know who might've put a sticker over the warning label on that box? Because we—"

I was interrupted by the shrill buzz of a cell phone. Anson's, to be exact.

He yanked it out, glanced at the screen, and let out a yip of anxiety. Then he scurried off without a backward glance.

"Hey!" Frank called, hurrying after him.

"Give it up, bro," I advised as I followed. "That guy's wound so tight he'll never hear you."

Frank sighed. "You're right. I can't believe someone like that even has time to notice Anya's alive. Let alone concoct some nasty plot to off me and win her heart or whatever."

"Yeah. So maybe it wasn't him. Maybe it was whoever *told* him to have you move that box."

"Exactly what I was thinking. But how do we figure out who that was, since Anson doesn't even seem to remember?"

"He mentioned a couple of people," I said. "Scorch is probably safe to cross off the list. But what about Jaan?"

Frank looked grim. "I know we talked about him before," he said. "But what's his motive for targeting me? He knows I'm not really her boyfriend. Plus, Jaan's the one who called in ATAC in the first place."

My mind raced ahead, figuring out the possibilities. "What if he's already regretting his decision to cast an unknown actress as his title character—especially one who's having trouble embracing the role of a tough action chick?"

"Yeah. So?" Frank countered. "Why wouldn't he just fire her and hire someone else?"

"That's what *you* would do, Mr. Logical," I told him. "But that's because you're not some big-name movie director with an even bigger ego. Maybe he's got too much pride to admit he made a mistake. So he starts sabotaging his lead actress, scaring her into wanting to quit. And the last straw comes when—"

"—the people he's brought in to protect her are killed in a fiery explosion on set." Frank looked thoughtful, though not fully convinced.

"Plus, we know Jaan loves publicity," I went on. "Just imagine the coverage if his lead quits halfway through and he ends up hiring a better-known actress, like Vance's girlfriend or whoever."

"Sounds pretty nuts," Frank said.

"Yeah. Nuts, just like Jaan." I shook my head, feeling a little freaked out by my new theory. "I mean, okay, I know it's far-fetched. But think about it, dude." I paused. "If it's true, he's not messing around. How are we supposed to deal if the person who brought us in on this mission is trying to kill us?"

An Exercise in Danger

Joe's theory about Jaan was pretty crazy. But he was right—so was Jaan.

"Guess we'd better look into it," I agreed. "If only to rule it out." I sent a quick text to HQ. The info came back almost immediately. I guess a famous movie director isn't too tough to research.

SUSPECT PROFILE

<u>Name</u>: Jaan St. John

<u>Hometown</u>: Beverly Hills, California

<u>Physical description</u>: Age 52, 5'7", 152 pounds. Salt-and-pepper hair, short grayish beard, bright blue eyes.

Successful director of numerous feature films. Most recently renowned for award-winning independent docudrama Milady.

<u>Background:</u> St. John worked in Europe for years, moving to Hollywood at age 35. He has earned a reputation as a genial eccentric. Also known for going over budget.

<u>Suspicious behavior:</u> Possibly instructing a production assistant to set up a deadly explosive "accident" (unconfirmed).

<u>Suspected of:</u> Trying to scare Anya into quitting her role as Deathstalker.

<u>Possible motives:</u> Saving face after realizing that Anya isn't up to the job; creating publicity for the film by replacing her with a marquee name in the middle of production.

Joe scanned the info. "Nothing too surprising here," he said. "I guess we know why Stan's always watching the money stuff so closely, though. Sounds like Jaan's not too good at staying on budget."

"Yeah, but that part's not our problem." I

pocketed my phone. "Come on, let's go talk to Jaan."

We reached his office just as he stepped out the door. Zolo was with him.

"Check it out," Zolo said when he spotted us. "It's Anya's loving boyfriend and his loyal sidekick."

"Have you heard how Scorch is doing?" I asked Jaan. Now that he was here in front of us, I was finding it even harder to believe he could be trying to kill anyone. He might be a little nutty, true. But it was hard to imagine a more mild-mannered nut.

Jaan stroked his close-cropped beard solemnly. "I just got off the phone with the hospital," he said. "Scorch will recover. But it will be a long, difficult road. I'm afraid we'll have to manage without him for quite a while."

"If you play with fire, you eventually get burned," Zolo commented softly.

"That's enough, my child," Jaan chided him gently. "This is no time for joking around."

Zolo shrugged. "I wasn't joking around. It's just a saying. Scorch said it all the time, remember?"

Okay, weird. But that was Zolo for you. The guy's social filter was seriously out of whack.

"Are you coming to watch our character class, my boys?" Jaan asked Joe and me.

"Character class?" Joe echoed. "What's that?"

"One of Jaan's crazy acting exercises," Zolo explained. "Like when he tries to make us all pretend to be trees and stuff."

Jaan chuckled. "Something like that, I'll admit," he said. "I do enjoy challenging my actors. But today—well, given Scorch's terrible accident, I thought we could all use a distraction."

Joe and I traded a glance. Sounded like we weren't going to have a chance to get Jaan alone right now. But maybe this was our chance to talk to some of the other actors.

"Sounds interesting," I said. "Lead the way."

We followed Jaan and Zolo across the set. When we reached the actors' trailers, Jaan knocked on several doors.

"Playtime, children!" he sang out. "Let's go!"

Vivian stuck her head out of Harmony's trailer. A moment later she and Harmony emerged to join us. Vance and Buzz came out of their trailers. A few of the adult actors appeared next. Finally Anya joined the group as well.

Then we all moved on. All around us, the crew was still working hard to dismantle the set. Some of the trailers had disappeared, leaving big chunks of space open with only temporary fencing keeping out the outside world. Since that outside world consisted of the Great Lawn in Central Park, there were plenty of people passing by. Many of them paused to cast curious looks inside.

Anya was walking between me and Joe. We made sure to downplay the accident with Scorch. She peered past me at the onlookers beyond the fence, her expression nervous.

"Deathstalker!" one of those onlookers called out to Anya. "You're gorgeous!"

Vivian caught up to us. "Maybe you should go over and sign a few autographs, dear," she advised Anya. "Your fans expect it."

"Oh." Anya gulped, looking nervous. "Um, are you sure we have time for that right now?"

It was pretty obvious that she didn't want to do it. But Harmony, Zolo, and Buzz had already stepped over to say hi to their own adoring fans among the crowd.

"Come on, baby." Vance put a protective arm around Anya's shoulders. "Stick with me, and I'll show you how to wow a crowd."

He dragged her toward the fence. The rest of us waited while the actors signed autographs and posed for cell phone photos.

"Looks like Anya's catching on," Joe commented as we watched her pose with a beaming woman holding a baby.

"Indeed." Jaan smiled proudly. "I knew she'd rise to the challenge of this role. The girl is a natural star in the making. She just needs to embrace that and she'll be fine."

I shot him a look. Jaan had always been Anya's biggest supporter. It was hard to believe he could really be our culprit.

But maybe that was what made him so dangerous. Who would believe the kindly old film director would sabotage his rising star? Let alone try to kill a pair of undercover agents . . .

"That's all, folks," Vance said loudly, snapping me out of my thoughts. "We've got to go. But make sure you all come out to support the film!"

He and the other actors turned away. Some of the fans groaned with disappointment, while others cheered.

Then, suddenly, Vance spun around to face them again. "Hey!" he yelped, slapping a hand to his own face. "Who did that?"

"Who did what?" asked Buzz, who was beside him.

Vance looked outraged. "Someone SPIT on me!" he shouted. "How dare you? I demand to know which disgusting moron just SPIT on me!"

Jaan hurried over, looking mildly alarmed. "Oh,

dear," he said. "I'm sure you must be mistaken. Perhaps a passing pigeon, hmm?"

"No way!" Vance stamped his foot. Yeah, literally. I didn't even know people actually did that. "I know when I'm being SPIT on, man!"

Joe and I scanned the crowd, on full alert. By now all the onlookers were staring at Vance. But nobody stepped forward to take credit for the spitting.

"Come on, Vance," Harmony said with a sigh. "Let's just get going."

"Yes, let's." Jaan stuck a hand into his pocket and pulled out about a dozen of those promo scorpion key chains. "Thanks for coming, folks!" he sang out, tossing them over the fence. The fans scrambled to catch them as we moved on.

"Think that spit could've been meant for Anya?" Joe whispered to me, looking at Vance, who was still complaining loudly as he walked between Jaan and Vivian.

"Maybe," I replied. "*If* there was any actual spitting, that is."

"You think he's lying?"

"Who knows? The guy clearly likes being the center of attention." I glanced at Anya. "With everything that's been going on around here lately, maybe he's feeling ignored."

Joe grinned. "Good point, bro."

Soon we reached an area near the rear gate. I was surprised when Jaan announced that this was the site of the acting exercise. The place was cluttered with all kinds of stuff waiting to be loaded onto trucks for the move to the Empire State Building— camera and sound equipment, random props and pieces of furniture, stacks of half-packed boxes, rolling racks of clothes, and more.

But I understood once he explained what the exercise was all about. It was something he called a Trust Walk. The actors would be divided into teams of two. One member of each team would be blindfolded, while the other teammate led him or her around.

"This is how we bond, by gaining trust in one another, hmm?" Jaan explained. "I want the guides to be creative in finding ways to build this trust. Lead your teammates here and there, helping them identify obstacles by touch. Perhaps even guide them in walking backward or skipping or jumping or stepping over things. Make them feel comfortable trusting you in any situation!"

Most of the actors just shrugged and nodded. I guess they were used to Jaan's crazy ideas by now.

But Anya looked nervous. "Do we really have to

be totally blindfolded?" she asked. "I don't like the sound of that."

"It will be fine, my child," Jaan assured her. "You can pair up with Harmony—you know she'll take good care of you. How's that, hmm?"

Harmony stepped toward her. "I'll wear the blindfold first if you want, Anya," she said. "You'll see—this'll be fun!"

Anya bit her lip, then agreed. "Okay. I guess I'll give it a try."

"Of course you will. If you can be the lead in a film that'll be seen by millions of people, you can surely lead Harmony around a private set for a few minutes, can't you, my dear?" Vivian grabbed a blindfold from Jaan and bustled over. She tied it over Harmony's eyes, then carefully fluffed the young actress's blond hair out around her face.

Joe and I stood beside Jaan and Vivian and watched while the Trust Walk began. There were six or seven other pairs besides Anya and Harmony. Zolo was partnered with Buzz. Vance was teamed up with one of the adult actors. I didn't pay much attention to the rest.

At first everyone was pretty tentative. The blindfolded partners kept their arms out in front of them, moving as slowly as possible. The leaders tugged at them, leading them here and there.

"Ouch!" Harmony yelped as she half tripped over a stray board. Then she giggled. "Hey Anya, watch the footing, okay? I just stubbed my toe!"

Anya looked sheepish. "Sorry!"

"Better your toe than your face, right?" Zolo called out from nearby. He was the blindfolded half of his partnership. Just then he tripped over a loose electrical cord and almost wiped out. "Hey!" he complained to his partner, Buzz. "You're supposed to be guiding me, Broadway Boy."

Buzz just laughed. "Hey Anya, want to trade partners?" he asked. "I won't blame you if you say no. I mean, we all know how tough it is to keep Zolo in line. Just ask anyone in Hollywood!"

That made everyone laugh, including Zolo. "Just watch it, okay?" he told Buzz. "Otherwise I'll make you pay when it's your turn."

Anya giggled. "Now you're in trouble, Buzz!" she warned. Then she glanced over at Harmony. "Oops, look out!" she exclaimed, grabbing the other actress's arm just in time to steer her around a large box of scripts.

Things went on like that for a while. Based on the giggles and playful comments from the participants, it was a lot more fun to do than it was to watch. Even Anya seemed pretty relaxed.

"This is a wonderful exercise for building

teamwork," Jaan came over to tell us. "Actors can become so involved in their own craft that they forget to connect with their costars. This forces them to forge those connections."

"Hmm." I tried to sound interested. But I wasn't too focused on theories of acting just then. I was distracted by the thought that this guy might want me and my brother dead. "Listen, about that explosion earlier. We're wondering if it's connected to our mission here."

Jaan glanced at me, one eyebrow raised quizzically. "Do you think so, my boy?" he said. "I mean, I suppose you two are the experts at that sort of thing. But you need to understand that Scorch's line of work can be quite dangerous, especially when explosives are involved. I imagine it was merely a misunderstanding—an unhappy accident caused by the chaos of the move."

An unhappy accident, huh? I glanced at Joe. He rolled his eyes. Yeah, we both would've been pretty unhappy if those explosives had gone off in our arms.

Just then Jaan turned away from us and whistled sharply. "Time to switch roles!" he called out. "Partners, trade those blindfolds!"

I glanced at Anya, wondering if she was going to protest again. But I guess leading Harmony around must've given her confidence or something. She looked pretty cheerful as she wrapped the blindfold around her head.

"Take it slow, okay?" she begged with a nervous giggle as Harmony took her by the arm. "I'm new at all this, remember?"

The Trust Walk started up again. I was getting impatient. We weren't accomplishing anything here, and Jaan seemed kind of distracted.

Harmony was giggling as she helped Anya sit down in a folding chair in the shade of a large metal camera crane. "Be right back!" she trilled playfully. "Don't go anywhere!" Then she hurried away, leaving Anya sitting there blindfolded and smiling.

I turned to Joe. "Let's sneak off and poke around while everyone's busy here," I murmured.

He nodded. We sidled away a few steps, then paused to see if anyone noticed.

Jaan didn't even glance our way. He was watching as Vance led his partner around backward, snorting with laughter every time the guy stumbled.

"I think we're good to go," Joe whispered.

We turned and walked off. But we'd gone only a few steps when we heard Zolo let out a shout.

"Anya!" he cried. "Get out of the way!"

I spun around. For a second all I saw was Anya sitting there on her chair, still blindfolded. Was Zolo just messing with her or something?

Then I heard Joe gasp. He'd already seen it— the huge, heavy camera crane toppling over—right toward Anya!

Changes

"Anya! Get out of the way!" Zolo shouted.

I glanced back—and gasped. Anya had been sitting right beside this ginormous camera mounted on a huge metal frame. A second ago it had been just standing there. Now it was about to fall and crush her! I sprinted toward her as fast as I could. But I could already see it was going to be too late. I was just too far away. So was Frank; I could hear him right behind me.

Luckily, one person was closer. Zolo.

He leaped forward, hitting Anya's shoulder with his own like some tiny, demented linebacker. The blow sent Anya flying off her chair.

"Oof!" she grunted as she hit the ground hard.

CRASH!

The giant camera hit the ground even harder. It missed Anya by a good three or four feet. And Zolo by about six inches.

"Whoa." Frank skidded to a stop beside me, staring. "That was close."

"Too close." I looked around. Jaan was racing toward Anya, babbling something about the exercise being over. "Think it was an accident?"

"Yeah," Frank said grimly. "As much of an accident as that explosion."

"Here we are." Frank climbed out of the taxi and squinted up at the Empire State Building towering overhead. "The new location."

It was the next morning. The move was complete. As soon as I jumped out of the cab, I spotted a familiar jumble of fencing, trailers, and camera equipment blocking out about half a block of prime Manhattan real estate. Not to mention a full lane of busy Fifth Avenue traffic.

"Let's go see what's crashed or exploded while we were sleeping," I said, only half kidding.

We had stuck around the old set as long as we could the day before. But it hadn't done much good. We couldn't find any clues to tell us how that camera dolly had tipped over.

So here we were and no closer to any answers. It was getting frustrating.

This set was a lot smaller than the last one. You'd think that would make it easier to find people, right?

Guess again. We wandered around for several minutes looking for Jaan. But he wasn't in his office, and we couldn't find him anywhere else. He wasn't answering his phone, either.

As we rounded a corner, we almost ran into Stan. He was leaning against a wall with his back to us, waving his free arm around wildly while ranting into his cell phone.

". . . and I couldn't believe it when Jaan told me," he was saying. "Like, *literally* couldn't believe it. I mean, do you know how much a camera like that costs? Do you?" Stan paused. "Well, neither do I, but I'm about to find out! Someone's looking at it now to see if it can be salvaged. But falling from that height? I'm not counting on it. . . ."

"Ouch," I whispered. "Think he's talking about that big camera that almost went smasho on Anya yesterday?"

Frank just nodded. Meanwhile Stan was still ranting.

". . . and it's bad enough dealing with all the delays—I expect that sort of thing. But then I've got this escalating budget, the ridiculous wind tunnel situation. . . . And of course the press isn't helping by questioning the casting every chance they get. . . ." He blew out a loud sigh. "I've seriously started to think it might be time for a change of personnel, or—"

He stopped short as he turned and noticed us standing there. Muttering something into the phone that we couldn't quite hear, he shot us a forced smile, then turned and hurried away.

"Wow," I said. "The dude sounded pretty annoyed."

"Yeah." Frank stared after the producer thoughtfully. "I hadn't really considered Stan a suspect. Until right now."

I knew what he meant. "He's got the access to anything he wants around the set," I said. "Plus, he was at the convention, so he could've done the stuff there."

"Motive?" Frank said.

"Obvious. He's the money guy, right? All about the box office."

Frank could see where I was going with this. "If all he cares about is making sure the movie's a financial success, he might think it would be better to have a big-name actress in the title role."

"Yeah. We already know casting Anya was all

Jaan's idea. And Stan doesn't seem too happy with a lot of Jaan's ideas." I reached into my pocket and pulled out the Deathstalker key chain Vance had tossed to Frank the other night. "Like these, for instance."

"So now he's talking about a change of personnel," Frank mused. "Like scaring Anya away from her role, maybe? But why wouldn't he just put his foot down, tell Jaan to fire her?"

I shrugged. "Got me, bro. I don't know how these things work. But I wouldn't want to be the one to tell Jaan to do anything."

Frank nodded and pulled out his phone. "Okay. It's worth keeping an eye on him. Just in case. I'll get the lowdown from HQ."

SUSPECT PROFILE

Name: Stan Redmond

Hometown: Pacific Palisades, California

Physical description: Age 61, 5'9", 170 pounds. Thinning gray hair, brown eyes, droopy jowls.

Occupation: successful film producer

Suspicious behavior: Complaining about the budget of the film; mentioning a "change of personnel."

After that we kept moving, trying to dodge stressed-out PAs and distracted crew members. We didn't see Stan again, but we finally found Jaan. He was at the fence by one of the gates.

Oh, and when I say "fence"? What I really mean is "pathetic strand of contractor's tape attached to some posts." Yeah, I could see why Anya wasn't so confident about this new set. It wasn't exactly high security.

Anyway, Jaan was signing autographs for a bunch of college-age dweebs wearing lots of black and serious expressions. You didn't have to be an ATAC agent to guess that they were film students.

"Can we talk to you?" Frank asked Jaan.

"Hmm?" The director glanced up from scribbling his name on a student's international film magazine. "Oh yes, I suppose so. Of course. Please excuse me, my fine young people. Duty calls."

He gave a little bow to the students, then wandered after us. "Did the crew have anything to say about that camera that fell over yesterday?" Frank asked him.

"The camera? No, no, I don't think so." Jaan sounded distracted. "But listen, my boys. How is your mission coming along? Is there any progress to report?"

"We're working on a few leads," I said. "Investigating a few suspects."

Okay, that was true. I just wasn't about to mention that one of those suspects was *him*!

"Good." Jaan frowned. "Because I'm starting to worry that our Anya is becoming fed up."

"Fed up?" Frank echoed. "What do you mean?"

Jaan sighed loudly, passing a hand over his face. "I suppose I'd better tell you," he said. "I just had a serious discussion with Anya and Vivian."

"Vivian? What's she got to do with this?" I felt a moment of panic. "Wait, she doesn't know what we're really doing here, does she?"

"No, nothing like that," Jaan said. "She's trying to help Anya—a stand-in, if you will—as Anya's real agent is still in California."

Frank looked confused. "A stand-in for her agent? What do you mean?"

"Well, you can imagine how frightening this has

been—that camera nearly falling on poor Anya," Jaan said. "Together with the earlier incidents, the fire and texts and such, and of course Scorch's unfortunate accident, which Anya seems to fear was no accident . . ."

It was always a little tough to follow Jaan's rambling way of speaking. But I was extra confused at the moment.

"So what are you saying?" I asked.

Jaan sighed again. "As things seem to be escalating, Anya has put her foot down," he said. "She says that no movie role is worth her life. If we cannot put a stop to all the trouble before the Big Apple Awards next week, she's off the project."

FRANK

7

Making Up Is Hard to Do

"We've got to talk to Anya about this," Joe said as Jaan hurried off.

I nodded. "Let's find her."

We tracked her down in the makeup trailer. She was sitting in one of the revolving chairs in front of a big mirror. A makeup artist was dabbing some kind of goop on her face.

"Bummer," Joe murmured, glancing around. "I guess we can't have a private chat with her anytime soon."

There were more than a dozen people in the trailer besides Anya. Various hairstylists and makeup artists, three or four teenage extras, a couple of actors getting turned into freaky-looking aliens, an attractive woman in her thirties I'd never seen before, a bodyguard or two, and Vance.

One of the extras spotted Joe. "Dude," he called. "Don't tell me you're actually going to be in a scene! Hurry up and get your face on—Jaan wants us ready to go as soon as Vance is done here."

"Oh," Joe said. "Um . . ."

I nudged him. "Better go with it, bro," I murmured, trying to hold back a smile. "Don't want to blow our cover, right?"

He shot me an evil look. "Right," he said. "I guess."

One of the makeup artists had heard the extra and came bustling over. "You're in this scene?" she asked Joe briskly. "You're late. Chair. Now."

She steered Joe firmly over to the mirror and planted him in an open seat between Vance and the thirtysomething woman. I grinned as I watched her expertly wipe down his face with a towelette, then start dabbing little spots of green stuff all over his face.

"Dude!" he exclaimed in alarm. "I'm supposed to be an extra, not an alien, right?"

"Relax, it's just concealer," the makeup artist said. "You've got a few red spots I need to fix. Now sit still."

The other extras looked over. "What's your

problem, buddy?" one of them said. "You act like you've never gotten made up for the camera before."

Joe grinned weakly. "Yeah, no," he said. "Uh—I was just kidding." He closed his eyes and braced himself.

I almost laughed out loud this time. He'd probably get me back for this later. But he'd been ragging me a lot about the whole "Anya's boyfriend" thing. This? Just a little payback.

"Easy with the eyeliner!" Vance told the woman working on his face. "I'm going to have a lot of close-ups today. My face has to look natural."

I looked over at him. He was peering critically into the mirror.

He caught my eye in the reflection and glanced back at me. "Did Anya tell you?" he asked. "We're filming the scene today when I confront her on the street right after I figure out her secret. It's probably the most dramatic scene in the entire film."

"Really?" Joe said.

He sounded skeptical. I knew how he felt. Considering the movie involved crashing alien spaceships, action-packed chases, and who knew what else, I sort of doubted some talky boy-girl scene was going to be the dramatic highlight.

"Yeah." Vance turned back around and stared smugly at his reflection. "By this time next year, I'll be practicing my acceptance speech for the Big Apple Awards. Mark my words."

Joe caught my gaze in the mirror and rolled his eyes. The eye rolling emphasized the eye shadow the makeup artist had just painted on his lids. I smirked.

Just then a skinny young man with dreadlocks hurried in. At first I thought he was holding a small black dog. Then I saw that it was a wig.

"Found it!" he said breathlessly, hurrying over to the thirtyish woman on Joe's other side.

"Thank goodness," the woman said. "I was afraid it got lost in the move."

With the help of a hairstylist, the woman carefully fitted the wig onto her head. The thick, wavy black hair tumbled over her shoulders, looking amazingly natural. I realized it looked just like Anya's hair.

I leaned toward Anya. "Who's that?" I whispered.

Anya glanced over. "Oh, that's Barb, my stunt double. She stands in for me in most of the fight scenes and takes the falls and scary stuff like that." She smiled at the woman, who'd glanced over at the sound of her name. "Her job is to look like me and do the dangerous stuff so I stay in one piece."

Barb chuckled. "That's right."

"Cool!" Joe looked impressed. And kind of goofy, considering the makeup artist was halfway through doing his eyes. "So what stunts are you doing today?"

"It's an easy day." Barb shrugged. "Just blocking a few fight moves and shooting some minor falls in front of the building. Tomorrow's the fun stuff—that's when I get to do the wind tunnel."

"Wind tunnel?" I said. Where had I heard that term lately? Oh yeah—Stan had mentioned it. "What's that all about?" I asked Barb.

"Yeah, Jaan mentioned he'd shoot your stunt stuff today if there was time, Barb," Vance broke in.

He'd been listening to the conversation and looked a little annoyed. Probably because we'd changed the subject away from his favorite topic: himself.

"But I'm not sure why you bothered to get dressed and made up so early," he went on. "You might get pushed back until tomorrow if my scene runs long. We'll definitely want to get as many takes as we need to make sure it's perfect."

Before Barb could respond, the door swung open again. This time a harried-looking woman with a clipboard rushed in.

"Change of schedule," she barked out. "The confrontation street scene's pushed back till tomorrow. We're shooting all the wind tunnel scenes today—Stan's orders."

"What?" Vance exclaimed. "You're kidding, right?"

"Do I look like I'm kidding?" the woman said. "Anya, your call time is in twenty minutes." Then she hurried out.

"Uh-oh," one of the alien actors said. "I wonder what that's all about."

"Wait, does this mean we're not shooting our scene today?" Joe asked. "Because if so, I'd better get this makeup off—I, um, have really sensitive skin. . . ."

Vance jumped to his feet. "This is totally stupid!" he shouted. "Why can't anything on this ridiculous movie just follow the freaking schedule?"

"Settle down, Vance," Barb began. "It's just one of those—"

"Don't tell me to settle down," he fumed. "I turned down several other very prestigious projects to do this film! And this is how I'm treated in return?" He slapped his hand down on the table so hard that a bottle of hairspray bounced off and landed on his foot. That seemed to set him off even more. With an angry howl, he swept one hand down the entire counter, sending tubes, bottles, hairbrushes, and half-full coffee cups flying.

"Vance!" Anya exclaimed, sounding alarmed.

But Vance was already stomping toward the door, muttering something about calling his agent.

"Whoa," one of the extras said when Vance was gone. "Talk about a temper!"

Barb shook her head. "That's actors for you." Then she looked apologetically at Anya. "Some actors, anyway."

Anya didn't answer. She looked upset. "Um, I think I need a moment," she said.

"Are you sure, sweetheart?" Her makeup artist was already digging around in the mess on the floor. "You heard what Kat just said—we're going to have to hurry to get you there on time."

"I'm sorry," Anya whispered, yanking off the bib that was protecting her Deathstalker catsuit while she got made up. "I'll be back in a minute."

"Might as well let her go," another makeup artist said with a sigh. "It'll take us a while to clean up this mess."

Moose followed Anya out of the trailer. Joe and I were right behind them.

"You all right?" Joe asked once we were all outside.

"I don't know." Anya shot a nervous look around.

From here, we were pretty visible to outsiders. Only that pathetic strand of tape separated us from the hordes of passing commuters and curious fans on the street. "Can we go to my trailer?"

Moose took her by the arm. "Come on," he rumbled.

He stayed outside while Joe and I went into the trailer with Anya. She kind of looked like she wished we'd stayed outside too.

"So we heard you're threatening to quit," Joe said as soon as we were alone with her. Mr. Tactful strikes again.

"Wouldn't you, if you were me?" she said. "I mean, how can anyone expect me to—"

She stopped short as a buzz came from her pocket. She pulled out her phone, glanced at it, and blanched. Then she quickly stuck it back in her pocket.

"Who was that?" I asked, instantly on alert.

She didn't meet my eye. "Nobody," she mumbled. "Just my agent."

Joe frowned. "Yeah, right," he said. "Look, Anya. We want to figure out who's harassing you as much as you do. But how can we do that if you're holding out on us?"

"I'm not," she said softly.

"Why should we believe that?" Joe was getting

fired up now. Uh-oh. When he got like this, it could be hard to stop him. "I'm starting to wonder if *you* should be on our suspect list! Have you been the one sabotaging yourself all along? Is that your sneaky way of getting out of this whole acting thing?"

"What?" Anya squeaked, looking startled. "No!"

Joe shrugged. "And now with this new ultimatum, I'm starting to wonder if you even *want* us to figure this out!"

I noticed that Anya was clenching her hands tightly in her lap. Her whole body looked like a coiled spring ready to explode.

Double uh-oh. Had Joe pushed her too far? Was she about to storm off just like Vance?

Then her shoulders slumped. "I'm sorry," she whispered. "You're right. I *have* been keeping something from you guys."

"Really?" I said, leaning forward.

She nodded and looked up. Tears glistened in her blue eyes. "But I'm positive it's not connected to the reason you're here," she said. "That's why I kept quiet. I didn't want to complicate the investigation. Or get him in trouble . . ."

Shooting the Breeze

"Him?" I blurted out, staring at Anya. "Him who?"

Anya sighed. "Big Bobby," she said.

"Big Bobby?" Frank sounded surprised. "Wait, you mean that's who just texted you? Why?"

"He's been trying to get in touch with me ever since Jaan fired him," she admitted. "And I'm pretty sure I know why."

She fished out her phone again. Frank read over my shoulder while I scanned the text message on the screen:

STILL NEED 2 TALK 2 U, ANYA. PLS GIVE ME 1 MORE CHANCE!

"Whoa," I said. "Sounds like he's begging for his job back."

Frank nodded. "He must figure if Anya asks Jaan to rehire him . . ."

"No," Anya said. "It's not about the job." She took a deep breath. "He, um, claims he's in love with me."

"What?" Frank exclaimed.

"Yeah." Anya bit her lip. "He's the one who sent me that rose the other night, too. Check it out."

She grabbed a little card off a table and handed it to us. Inside, a message was scrawled in messy handwriting:

> Since you won't see me, this rose is the
> only way I can show you how I feel.
> Love, BB

"Kind of creepy," I said.

"Yeah, I'm thinking it's a good thing we already have him on our suspect list," Frank added. "He sounds like some kind of stalker."

"No, it's not like that," Anya protested. "Please, don't be too hard on Big Bobby. I'm sure he's not connected with all the trouble."

"How do you know?" Frank asked, tossing the card back on the table.

"He's not like that," Anya said. "He's just a big, awkward kid."

"Yeah." I snorted. "*Really* big."

Anya smiled slightly. "No, really. He's barely out of high school and is kind of naive and sweet, just maybe a little confused. But I'm sure he'd never hurt me."

The trailer door swung open. A makeup artist stuck her head in.

"They need you back right away," she said.

"Okay." Anya glanced at us. "Coming?"

"We'll meet you in a while." I'd just caught a glimpse of myself in a mirror on the wall. It wasn't a pretty sight. Or maybe I should say it was a little *too* pretty. "Can I borrow your bathroom? I need to get this junk off my face."

She giggled. "Sure. But for the record, you look cute in eye shadow."

"Yeah, thanks a lot," I muttered as she hurried out after the makeup person.

"Come on, bro," Frank said. "No time to waste on primping."

I glanced at him. He looked worried and super geeky and responsible, as usual. But he was smirking a little too.

"This'll only take a minute." I headed for the open bathroom door.

Frank leaned on the door frame, watching me splash water on my face. "What do you think about this Big Bobby thing?"

"Dunno." I scrubbed at my eyeliner. Ow. I don't know how girls do it. "The rose thing and the texts are pretty crazy. But are they connected to the other incidents? If Big Bobby is in love with Anya, why would he set fire to her dressing room and do all that other stuff?"

"That's what I'm wondering. What's the motive?"

I blinked water out of my eyes, looking around for some soap. "Then again, we did see him at the convention," I went on. "So he totally could've rigged the microphone and set the other fire after he got fired."

"But if he loves Anya like he claims, why would he try to electrocute her?" Frank wondered. "Or try to kill her by pushing that camera over on her?"

"Yeah, that stuff doesn't make much sense." I grabbed a towel. "But maybe he was the one who tried to blow you up yesterday. He could be trying to get rid of the competition."

"Except how'd he get on set? He'd have to get through security."

"He might have enough friends on the crew to find a way in."

Frank nodded. "I guess you're right. We'll have to look into it. In the meantime, it couldn't hurt to start a dossier on him. I'll text HQ."

He sent the message. By then my face was looking mostly normal, so we headed out.

We were just in time to see a group of people hurrying past. They were walking toward the Empire State Building's entrance.

I spotted Barb and a couple of the alien actors among them. "What's going on?" I asked the stuntwoman.

"We're getting ready to start filming," she said. "Anya's still in makeup. But Stan's in some big hurry, so we're doing my scenes first."

Frank glanced around the busy city street. "Where's the wind tunnel?"

"Observation deck. Eighty-sixth floor." She gestured up.

Way up.

"Cool!" I said. "Come on, bro. Let's go watch."

Everyone entered the building and crammed into the elevators. "Hold the door!" someone called.

Frank stuck out his hand to stop the door from closing. Buzz rushed up and shoved himself in, panting.

"Whew!" he said. "Sorry I'm late."

"Are you in this scene too?" I asked.

Buzz shook his head. "I'm just here to watch today," he said. "I'm totally geeked to check out the wind tunnel."

"I didn't even know there was one in the Empire State Building," Frank said.

"There isn't usually," Buzz explained. "Jaan rented a portable one—it's what's known as a vertical wind tunnel, which is a little different from the ones used for researching aerodynamics and stuff like that. A huge fan blows air up powerfully enough to support a person's weight. That lets you sort of 'fly' in place, you know? They're used a lot for training skydivers."

I was surprised that Buzz knew so much about the wind tunnel if he wasn't even actually shooting in one. Then I remembered. His father was some kind of engineer. I guess it had rubbed off on Buzz. He was the one who'd figured out how someone had rigged Anya's microphone to electrocute anyone who touched it.

"Oh, right," Frank said. "We tried out one of those once. Remember, Joe?"

"Yeah." How could I forget? It had been during that crazy mission in an amusement park.

But this was no time for reminiscing.

"So what's the scene they're shooting?" I asked.

"And why is the wind tunnel on the observation deck?"

"Same answer to both questions, dude." Buzz grinned. "It's part of the final big action scene of the film—"

"Final?" I interrupted. "Wait, how can you be almost done with filming?"

Buzz chuckled, along with some of the other people crushed into the elevator with us. "Not even close," he said. "We shoot the whole movie out of order. It makes it hard to keep track of what's going on sometimes."

The elevator stopped, and the doors slid open. When we reached the deck, I finally got a look at the wind tunnel. It took up most of the open-air part of the observation deck. A padded base surrounded the huge fan. Thin netting was strung up around the sides.

"Good thing that netting's there." I glanced out over the panoramic view of New York City. "It'd really stink to fly a little too far to the left and end up flying through the air for real."

Buzz was still standing with us. "Yeah. Talk about a crash landing. No wonder Anya's nervous about her scenes. I'd be too." He grinned again. "But I'd still totally do it!"

"Wait, so Anya has to do the wind tunnel thing?"

I said. "Then what's the stuntwoman for?"

Buzz glanced over at Barb, who was chatting with Jaan over near the guardrail. "Oh, Barb is handling most of the action stuff," he said. "Anya just has to get up there long enough to shoot a few close-ups."

"So what's the scene they're shooting?" Frank asked.

"Like I said, it's the last big action sequence," Buzz replied. "Deathstalker catches up to the bad guys and ends up chasing them up the pinnacle."

"King Kong–style!" I put in.

Buzz nodded. "Yeah, pretty much. Anyway, they fight up there, and she ends up getting tossed off the building. The wind tunnel is how Jaan plans to make the falling parts and the midair fighting action look real." He shrugged. "Actually, it was my idea to use the wind tunnel. He was just going to do it all with green screens and stuff once we get back to Hollywood."

"Cool," I said.

"That's what Jaan said." Buzz grimaced. "But I hear Stan had a different reaction. I guess it's pretty expensive to rent one of these things and get it up here."

Yeah. If Stan was complaining about the price of some key chains, I could only imagine his reaction to the bill for this.

Actually, I could see his reaction for myself. I noticed Stan was standing nearby, watching everyone rush around getting ready for the filming. He looked less than thrilled.

Buzz wandered off for a closer look at the wind tunnel. I was still watching Stan.

"Let's go say hi to the money man," I told Frank.

"Good call. We might as well talk to all the suspects we can while we're up here."

When we reached Stan, he was checking his watch. "Oh," he said when he saw us. "Uh, it's Anya's boyfriend, right? Do you know if she's almost ready? We're already running behind."

"Sorry, I'm not sure," Frank said. "Last I heard she was still in makeup."

Stan swore softly. "At least the stuntwoman's here and ready to go," he commented, looking over at Barb.

"I bet this wind tunnel effect is going to look great on film," I said, trying to sound casual. "Must be kinda pricey, though, huh?"

"That's the understatement of the year!" Stan rolled his eyes so hard his irises almost disappeared. "Another one of Jaan's insane ideas. Can you believe he was planning to stretch out this shoot over the whole week? Give me a break! He must think this picture has an unlimited budget!"

"So now he's got to shoot it all in one day?" Frank asked.

Stan's frown faded, replaced by a smug smile. "That's right. I already arranged for the rental place to come pick it up tonight. Jaan will just have to deal with the change of schedule *and* the whimperings of his unpredictable leading lady. If he decides it's not worth it? Oh well."

His phone rang, and he stomped off to answer. Frank and I traded a look. But there was no time to discuss what we'd just heard. Jaan was calling for quiet on the set.

He looked kind of cranky. No wonder. Jaan was pretty mild-mannered, but he was used to getting his way.

I forgot about that as things got started. Barb was all decked out in her costume and wig. She looked so much like Anya that it was eerie.

Someone fired up the wind tunnel, and soon Barb was floating on her stomach like a skydiver. She started with a few flips and tumbles. It looked like she was just getting used to things.

"That looks awesome," I said to Frank as Barb did an elaborate kung-fu-style movement. "Think there's any chance Jaan'll let us give it a whirl when they're done?"

"Yeah. Dream on," Frank said.

Jaan whistled sharply. "Let's proceed!" he called, raising his voice to be heard above the roar of the huge fan powering the wind tunnel. "Barb, please begin with the free-fall tumbling, if you please."

"You got it, boss." The stuntwoman floated up a little higher.

"Hi," a voice said softly from right behind us.

I glanced back and saw Deathstalker herself standing there.

Okay, it was actually Anya. We hadn't really seen her in full costume and makeup yet.

"You look amazing!" I told her.

She stared past me. Jaan had called for action, and Barb was writhing around in the wind tunnel.

"How's it going so far?" she asked. "I can't believe I have to go in that thing next."

"Don't worry, I've been in one before," Frank assured her. "It's kind of fun. And very safe. See? There's netting all around in case you float out of the wind stream, and it's well braced so you don't have to worry that . . ." His voice trailed off and he took a step forward, staring at the lower part of the wind tunnel setup.

"What's wrong, bro?" I asked.

Instead of answering me, Frank let out a yell. "Stop!" he shouted, racing forward. "The safety netting—it's not attached on that side!"

But his warning was a half second too late. Because just then Barb finished a flip and bounced off the netting on the far side.

At least that's what she meant to do.

Instead, the netting gave way from the impact. It collapsed, sending the stuntwoman flying— right over the edge of the observation deck.

And eighty-six stories to the ground.

Message Received

"I still can't believe it," Anya moaned. "This is a nightmare!"

I knew how she felt. Joe and I had been sitting in her trailer, basically watching her freak out, for the past hour.

I was feeling pretty freaked out myself. "I wish I'd spotted that loose netting sooner," I mumbled for about the nine millionth time. "Maybe Barb would still be alive."

Joe stepped over to the window and pulled back the curtain to peek out. "Yeah," he said. "And half the news teams in the world wouldn't be circling like sharks out there."

"Poor Barb!" Anya sniffled, then shivered. "And

it's all my fault she's dead. I'm sure that messed-up netting was meant for me. I was supposed to shoot my part first."

She was probably right about that. But I wasn't about to say so.

"If it makes you feel any better, you almost certainly wouldn't have fallen to your death like she did," I pointed out instead. "Since you'd just be floating and not doing all those flips and stuff, you wouldn't have hit the net with that much velocity. So at worst you might've broken an arm when you hit the floor of the observation deck."

She shot me a dismayed look and didn't answer.

Oops. Guess it hadn't made her feel any better.

"Smooth, bro," Joe whispered. "Very smooth."

There was a knock on the door. Moose stuck his head in.

"The limo's here," he told Anya.

She jumped to her feet and grabbed her purse. "Finally," she said. "All I want to do is hide out in my hotel room. For about a year."

Once they were gone, I pulled out my phone. "Who are you calling?" Joe asked.

"Jaan. I want to see if the cops figured out what happened to that safety netting."

When Jaan answered, he sounded almost as

shaky as Anya. "It just doesn't make sense," he told me. "The police have questioned everyone, and nobody knows what went wrong. The crew insists they double- and triple-checked that safety netting when they helped set up the wind tunnel this morning."

"They're sure?" I asked.

"Absolutely. I fear someone must have tampered with it between setup and filming." Jaan sighed. "We left a couple of guards up there, of course, but perhaps . . ."

"Don't worry, we're working on some theories," I told him.

"We are?" Joe asked as I hung up.

"At least this narrows things down," I pointed out. I'd been thinking it through while watching Anya cry. "Only a limited number of people had access to the observation deck."

"Yeah. The same three dozen people as usual." Joe didn't sound too impressed. "Maybe it's time to have HQ run background info on the entire cast and crew."

That reminded me of something. I pulled out my phone again.

"HQ sent us the info we wanted on Big Bobby," I said.

SUSPECT PROFILE

Suspect: Robert "Big Bobby" Sterling

Hometown: Flagstaff, Arizona

Physical description: Age 20, 6'4", 260 pounds. Red hair, hazel eyes, very muscular.

Occupation: Bodyguard for the entertainment industry

Background: Graduated from high school as an average student. Moved to California with his then-girlfriend and stayed even after the relationship ended.

Employment history: Has held a series of jobs on movie sets, but most only for a short time—anywhere from a few days to a few weeks.

Suspicious behavior: Stalking Anya, sending unwanted messages and gifts. Was also witnessed threatening Jaan.

Suspected of: Pushing camera over to hurt Anya, sabotaging wind tunnel.

Possible motives: Revenge for being fired. Removing competition for Anya's affections. Frightening her either out of spite for not returning his interest and/or to make her seek his protection.

"Well I don't think he could have pushed over the camera. Someone would have seen and recognized him, but this part's kind of strange." I pointed to the stuff about Big Bobby's employment history. "Do you think it's because he's always late?"

"That's why Jaan fired him, I guess," Joe said. "Might be worth asking HQ to look into it more, though."

"I'm on it." I sent another quick text, then stood up. "Anyway, he should be an easy one to rule in or out. Let's go talk to people, find out if there's any way Big Bobby could've gotten access to that wind tunnel."

"Okay." Joe followed me out the door. "I still don't get why he'd try to hurt Anya if he claims to love her. But let's check it out."

We started questioning anyone we could find about who might have had access during the key time. Since we were supposed to be undercover, we tried to keep it subtle.

But I'm not sure it mattered. The mood was pretty somber around set. Everyone had heard about the accident.

"I'm starting to think this production is cursed," said the nervous PA, Anson, when we questioned him. "Everything keeps going wrong!"

"I hear you, bro." Joe smiled sadly at him. "But

listen, Anya wanted to, um, make sure her old bodyguard, Big Bobby, heard about this before it hit the news. Have you seen him lately?"

"Big Bobby?" Anson looked surprised. "Of course not. Jaan fired him a few days ago."

"Yeah, we know," I said. "But we figured he probably had friends here and maybe might stop in to visit—"

Anson was already shaking his head. "No way," he said firmly. "Jaan gave strict orders to the entire crew. We're supposed to contact him if we see Big Bobby anywhere near the set." He paused. "Besides, I'm pretty sure I heard some of the other bodyguards talking about how Big Bobby went back to Arizona right after he got canned. Like, to visit his family or something."

Interesting. The part about the visit home was new. But the rest pretty much matched what a couple of other people had already told us. It was starting to feel like we were spinning our wheels.

"Okay, thanks," I told Anson. "See you later."

"So I guess Big Bobby is out," Joe said as Anson hurried away. "Even if one or two people took pity on him and sneaked him in, there's no way someone else wouldn't see him before long. At his size he doesn't exactly blend into the background."

"Agreed. I'm thinking maybe Anya was right.

He might be stalking her or whatever, but he's not the one trying to hurt her."

"So who else is on the list? Jaan, Stan, Vance . . ."

"What about Zolo?" I put in. "Come to think of it, I haven't seen him all day. Was he even on the set today?"

"I didn't see him either. And that dude's hard to miss."

"There's someone else who was around, though," I pointed out. "Buzz."

"Oh man." Joe shook his head. "Buzz seems like such a cool guy. Do you really think he could be our culprit?"

I stepped past a shed of camera equipment, staring at the line of actors' trailers up ahead. "We've got to consider every possibility," I said. "And Buzz was definitely around during the wind tunnel disaster. Even though he had the day off from filming and didn't need to be there."

"True. He even told us the wind tunnel was all his idea." Joe frowned. "Has he been around for any of the other incidents?"

I thought back over the list. "He was around during the Trust Walk. And he was at the convention."

Joe gulped. "Right. And he seemed to know all about how someone might've rigged that electrocuting microphone, remember?"

"Yeah. Would he really be smart enough to set that up—and stupid enough to let us know he had the know-how to do it?"

"Got me. But I'm thinking we'd better get some more info on Mr. Broadway."

"Yeah." I pulled out my phone.

After texting HQ, we started wandering around again. It was getting harder to find people to interview. The set seemed to be shutting down for the day, even though it wasn't that late.

"We're not getting anywhere here, bro," Joe said at last. "Maybe we should head back to the hotel. We can pick up again first thing in the a.m."

"Okay."

We headed for the gate. As we passed the dressing room trailers, a door flew open. Vance emerged, looking wild eyed and red faced.

"Uh-oh," Joe whispered. "Looks like he hasn't simmered down yet."

"Um, hi," I greeted Vance cautiously. "You okay?"

He spun and stared at me. "What?"

"You look kind of upset, dude," Joe put in.

Vance glared at him. "Have you seen Jaan?" he demanded. "Or my agent? I seriously need to talk to someone."

"I don't think Jaan's around," I said. "I don't know about your agent."

"Did something happen?" Joe asked.

"None of your beeswax," Vance snapped.

"Come on, man," Joe said. "We're all on edge after what happened earlier. But if you tell us what's up, maybe we can help you track down Jaan."

Vance looked skeptical. But finally he shrugged and pulled out his cell phone.

"Here's what's up," he told us. "I just got a threatening text from an unknown sender on my private cell phone!"

Surprising Secrets

U h-oh. Another threatening message? I traded a look with Frank. Was someone targeting the other actors now too?

It took a while to convince Vance to show us the threatening message. I kind of got the feeling he was planning to make it an exclusive to the *New York Times* or something.

But finally he let us see. The text was in all caps: HEY VANCEY PANTS, U R AS FAKE AS YR FAKE CHARACTER, PORKER DORKERON! ALL TRU DS FANS H8 U!

Okay, I kind of got it. Vance's character, Parker Oberon, was Deathstalker's love interest, but he wasn't in the Deathstalker comics. The screenwriters had invented him for the movie to add more romance. Some of the fans at the convention had been pretty worked up about it. Whoever had sent this message seemed to be too.

"Oh," Frank said. "Um, that's pretty low. But it doesn't really sound like a threat."

"Easy for you to say!" Vance exclaimed.

"We could take the phone and try to get it traced if you want," I offered.

He looked at me suspiciously. "Why would I trust some random extra from Minnesota to do that?" he said. "Are you trying to steal my contacts list and sell it to the *National Enquirer* or something?"

Okay, I *so* wouldn't do that. But I realized my offer probably did seem kind of random. Undercover, remember?

Frank gave me a warning look. "I'm sure Joe meant we could help you find Jaan so he could contact the police," he said.

"Whatever," Vance said. "Whoever gave this creep my number better hope I never find them. Because I don't need this kind of stress!"

We soothed him as best we could. Then we took off.

"Well?" I asked Frank as we hurried through the

gate. "Think Vance's message is connected to our mission?"

"I don't know. It's not threatening. It just seems to be making fun."

"Yeah. It kinda seemed like a totally different sender." Then another idea occurred to me. "Hey, what if Vance sent that text to himself?"

"You mean to throw off suspicion?" Frank looked thoughtful. "I guess it's possible—*if* he's the one who's been harassing Anya."

I grinned. "It would totally explain how the 'sender' got his private number."

"Funny," Frank said. "But now that you mention it, maybe we should think about which of our other suspects *would* have Vance's number."

I kicked at a gum wrapper on the sidewalk. We were walking uptown, heading in the general direction of our hotel.

"Are you thinking about Buzz?" I asked.

"Mostly," Frank admitted. "Although most of the others probably have it too."

We paused at the corner, waiting for the light to change. I thought about Buzz. Nice guy. Smart. Friendly. Talented.

"What would Buzz have to gain from all this?" I wondered.

"From the Vance thing? Who knows," Frank said as we crossed the street. "But he's a smart guy. Maybe he's trying to make it less obvious that Anya's the real target."

"I get that," I said. "But why would he want Anya to quit the film? He makes it sound like he doesn't even care that much about being in the movies. Like he's totally happy on Broadway."

"Yeah, but what if he's lying? This is his first big movie role. One that could make him a star. And movie stars make a lot more money than stage actors."

"They're a lot more famous, too." I nodded. "If he thinks this is his one big shot to go Hollywood, he might be worried that Anya could hurt the film's chances of being a hit."

"It kind of makes sense," Frank said.

I sighed. "Yeah. I just don't want to believe Buzz's Mr. Nice Guy personality is an act. He's, like, the most normal person on this entire production."

Frank stifled a yawn. "Whatever. I'm too tired to think about it anymore right now. Let's find something to eat, then get some rest. With the way this mission is going, we need to be ready for anything tomorrow."

• • •

"Remind me again, bro," I told Frank. "Why'd we have to get here at the crack of dawn? Anya's call time isn't for, like, two hours."

We were back at the temporary location set at the Empire State Building. It was early—too early, if you asked me. Which Frank hadn't.

"Seven thirty is hardly the crack of dawn," Frank said. "And we don't have any time to lose, especially if Anya is really going to quit if things aren't solved before the Big Apple Awards."

He had a point. Not that I was about to admit it.

"There's one of our suspects now," I said, spotting Zolo just as he disappeared behind a trailer.

"Good. Let's go talk to him."

When we rounded the corner, we got a surprise. Zolo wasn't alone. Anya was with him.

The two of them were in a small, private spot surrounded on all sides by trailers, sheds, and a large Dumpster. A couple of exercise mats were laid out on the sidewalk. On one of them, Anya was striking some kind of yoga pose. I think it was Downward-Facing Dog. Not sure. I always zoned out when Mom started her yoga talk.

"What are you doing here?" Frank blurted out.

"Uh-oh!" Zolo smirked. "Do I detect a note of jealousy? Don't worry, man. I'm not out to steal your girlfriend."

Anya looked up at us. She still looked sad. But not as freaked out as yesterday.

"Don't tease Frank, Zolo," she said, breathing out slowly between words. "You're supposed to be achieving inner peace, remember?"

"Oh, right." Zolo stepped onto his own mat and started to stretch. "You two want to join us?"

"Maybe another time," I said. "Since when do you guys do yoga together?"

Anya dropped her pose and sat up. "It's only been a couple of days," she explained. "Zolo noticed I was stressed and offered to teach me."

Zolo had struck his own pose by now. Cobra, I think.

He looked ridiculous. But sort of peaceful.

"Yoga's what keeps me sane in Hollywood," he said, sounding a lot less sardonic than usual. "I figured it might help Anya, too."

"Okay," I said. "Um, enjoy."

Frank and I wandered off. "Wow," I said when we were out of earshot. "I never would've pegged Zolo as some kind of Zen yoga master."

"Me neither," Frank said. "But he's looking like less of a suspect all the time."

"I know. He's still a total weirdo, but he hasn't really done anything suspicious since we've been watching him." I shrugged. "Well, other than trying to listen in when we were talking about being ATAC agents."

"And we're not even sure about that," Frank put in. "Plus, he actually seemed to be helping Anya just now. She looked a lot calmer than I expected her to be after what happened yesterday."

"That reminds me—he wasn't around for the wind tunnel thing, either."

"I think it's probably safe to move him to the bottom of the list," Frank said. "At least until we check out some of the others."

"Like Jaan?" I glanced forward, realizing we were nearing his office.

"Yeah. He might actually be here this early," Frank said. "Maybe he'll even have time to talk to us."

Before I could respond, the office door swung open. Vance bounded out, grinning from ear to ear. Right behind him was a gorgeous girl with wavy dark hair and bright green eyes.

My eyes widened. I recognized the girl right away. Why wouldn't I? I'd probably seen half a dozen of her movies.

Vance spun around and grabbed her by the hands. "Just you wait, baby," he bragged loudly. "That part will be yours before you know it!"

FRANK

11

Just Business

"Let's get out of here," I hissed, grabbing Joe's arm.

I didn't want Vance to see us. That pretty brunette had to be his girlfriend, Amy Alvaro. If he realized we'd overheard what he'd just said . . .

"Hey!" Vance's smile turned into an angry scowl.

Uh-oh. Too late. He'd just spotted us standing there.

He came stomping toward us. "What are you doing skulking around the set this early?" he demanded.

"We're not skulking," Joe said. "We're just, uh, morning people."

If it hadn't been such a tense situation, I would have laughed. Joe, a morning person? Yeah, right.

"Calm down, Vance." Amy strolled forward to join us. "What's the big deal? Everyone already knows I want to play Deathstalker."

"Is that what you're doing here?" Joe asked. "Are you still trying to get the part?"

Amy looked him over coolly. "So what if I am? The buzz all over Hollywood is that Anya is going to be a spectacular failure. There was just a story on one of the big entertainment blogs about it yesterday, with an anonymous source on the set confirming that everyone here thinks so." She shrugged. "So what's wrong with giving Jaan another option in case he wants it? It's just business."

"An anonymous source, huh?" Joe shot Vance a disgusted look.

Vance raised both hands. "Don't look at me, buddy," he said. "I didn't do it, I swear. I mean, sure, I think it's nuts that Jaan cast an unknown with zero experience. And sure, I think my girl here would make an outstanding Deathstalker."

"Thanks, baby," Amy put in.

"But I've got nothing personal against Anya," Vance went on. "I wouldn't actually try to sabotage her by leaking that kind of story." He shook his head. "In fact, ever since I got that creepy text yesterday, I have even more sympathy for her."

"What do you mean?" I asked.

"You know—because she got some texts like that too." Vance stared at me. "You must know about that, right? I mean, you're her boyfriend."

"Of course I know about it," I said. "How do *you* know about it?"

"Heard about it somewhere. You know how gossipy movie sets can be." He paused and looked us over. "Or maybe you don't know. Anyway, I forget who told me. Maybe one of the makeup people, or a PA or someone. Who cares? It's true, right? Everyone probably knows about it by now."

That was news to me and Joe. We'd thought Anya and Jaan were the only ones who knew about those texts.

Amy was starting to look bored. "Let's go get breakfast," she said with a tug on Vance's arm. "I'm hungry."

"Okay. Gotta stop at my dressing room first." Vance started to leave, then paused and looked back. "But hey—you don't need to mention this to Anya, all right? Like I said, we're not trying to hurt her feelings or anything. It's not personal."

"Right," Joe said. He sounded a little sarcastic, but Vance didn't seem to notice. He waved, then took off with Amy.

"Come on," I told Joe. "At least now we know Jaan's in there. Let's go talk to him."

Soon we were sitting in Jaan's office. I'd almost forgotten how weird the place was. There were all kinds of bizarre artifacts decorating the place. A shrunken head hanging from the ceiling fan. Exotic insects mounted on velvet. Tribal weapons decorating the walls. Even a huge stuffed crocodile head. You'd think the guy was an explorer instead of a movie director.

But I wasn't too interested in the decor just then. I was looking at Jaan. He seemed tired. There were huge bags under his eyes, and he was pale behind his beard.

"How can I help you boys?" he asked.

"We just ran into Vance outside," Joe said. "And Amy Alvaro."

Jaan looked at him. "I suppose you've guessed why they were here, hmm?"

"You're not actually thinking of replacing Anya with Amy, are you?" I asked.

"I hope not!" Joe put in. "That would be like letting the bad guys win!"

Jaan chuckled briefly. "Don't worry, that's not my style," he said. "I have no intention of recasting the part. Certainly not with Amy Alvaro—she's a bit too old to be convincing in the role." He shot a slightly nervous glance toward the door. "Er, but don't tell her I said so, will you?" he added with a wink. "She'd probably chop off my head with my own genuine antique Qing dynasty sword if I told her that." He gestured toward one of the impressive-looking weapons displayed near his desk.

Joe and I laughed politely. But I suspected Jaan was only half joking. Amy seemed like a pretty tough cookie. I understood why Jaan didn't want to make her mad.

"So Anya's part is safe?" Joe asked.

"Of course." Jaan leaned back in his chair. "I still believe in Anya. I just hope she still believes in herself, given all that's happened lately."

I wasn't sure what to say to that. Before I could figure it out, we all heard a shrill scream.

"What was that?" Joe was on his feet instantly.

So was I. "It sounded like it came from pretty close by."

We both raced for the door. At first we didn't see anyone outside.

Then Joe glanced toward the cast's trailers. "Look!" he cried, pointing.

I spun around and gasped.

Vance was standing near his trailer. He was clutching his head and moaning as blood streamed down his face.

Deadly Mementos

F rank sprinted toward Vance. "Don't move!" he shouted. "What happened?"

I followed, already looking around for an answer. Vance was standing near the trailers. He was also near one of the spots where all that separated the set from the city street was a thin line of caution tape and a couple of sawhorses.

It was so early that most of the people passing by barely paused to look in. They just clutched their briefcases and coffee cups and hurried past. Even the tabloid TV people who'd been hanging around since Barb's death weren't there yet.

But one person was standing at the rope looking in. A nerdy-looking teenager. Skinny.

Gangly. Faded monster-movie T-shirt.

The kid was standing there with his mouth hanging open. Staring at Vance.

I glanced over. Frank and Amy were both with Vance now. Amy was pressing a napkin or something to his head, while Frank dialed his cell phone. Vance was whining like a little girl.

Okay, things seemed to be under control over there.

Then I noticed something on the ground nearby. The morning sun glinted off it.

It was one of those expensive metal promo key chains shaped like a scorpion. When I glanced at Nerdy McNerderson again, I saw another key chain dangling from his hand.

"You!" I yelled as he started sidling away. "Stop!"

The kid's eyes widened. Dropping the second key chain, he broke into a run.

So did I. I ducked under the tape, caught up in about three steps, and tackled him. He went down with a pathetic whimper.

"Why'd you do it?" I shouted into his ear.

He started to sob. "I'm sorry!" he babbled. "I didn't think I'd actually hit him. Or that he'd bleed like that even if I did!"

I heard footsteps hurrying toward us. It was Frank.

"Vance is okay," he reported. "It's just a nick on the forehead. You know, one of those shallow head wounds that can bleed like crazy . . ."

"Yeah." I grabbed the key chain the kid had dropped. "One of the pincers must've hit him just right."

Frank glanced at it, then at the kid. "So you threw one of those things at Vance?" he demanded. "What else have you been up to? Burning posters and electrocuting people with microphones, maybe?"

The kid looked confused. "Huh?"

"At FanCon," I prompted, hauling him to a sitting position. "Were you there?"

"FanCon? I wish!" the kid said. "My parents wouldn't let me go."

"You sure about that?" I leaned closer, trying to look threatening. "Might as well tell the truth, man. Because if you're the one who's been trying to scare Anya, the cops will get it out of you sooner or later."

"Scare Anya? What? Look, I don't know what you're talking about." The kid grabbed his sunglasses, which had fallen off when I tackled him. "I love Anya—she's going to be a totally awesome Deathstalker! My only problem is with *him*." He pointed at Vance. "His stupid character shouldn't even exist! I mean, I can't believe they thought they'd get away with it. What, do they think we Deathstalker fans have, like, short-term memory problems or something?"

He kept rambling on. But I kind of stopped listening. This was all way too familiar. The kid was giving me flashbacks to that convention, and all the fans who took this whole Deathstalker thing way too seriously.

We finally got him to quit complaining about the addition of Parker Oberon and questioned him a little more. He admitted to spitting on Vance earlier and sending him that obnoxious text message—apparently some super-hacker techie friend of his had worked his magic to acquire the digits.

But he had no clue what we were talking about with the other stuff. It figured.

We should've known it wouldn't be that easy.

Later that day Frank and I watched some filming on the street just outside the Empire State Building. They were shooting Vance's big dramatic scene, the one that had been pushed back from yesterday. The makeup people were geniuses. You couldn't see the scratch on his forehead at all, even in close-up.

Not that Vance let anyone forget it was there.

About every ten minutes, he'd stop the action, pretending to feel faint.

"Is this dude a drama queen or what?" I murmured after about the fifth time.

Frank glanced over. "Guess he chose the right job," he quipped.

Nearby, Jaan was perched on a director's chair—yeah, there's a reason they call them that—watching the action.

"Okay, Vance," he called out. "Take five and we'll try again. All right, my boy?"

Vance hurried over to his assistant, who handed him a water bottle. We stepped over to Jaan.

"What happened to that fan?" Frank asked the director. "Did you convince Vance not to press charges?"

"Thankfully, yes." Jaan glanced around to make sure nobody was close enough to hear us. "The young man has no prior record of any sort of bad behavior. It would have been poor publicity to prosecute over a silly little incident like that." He smiled ruefully. "Though I didn't phrase it quite like that when I spoke to Vance, of course."

"Good," Frank said. "With that out of the way, maybe we'll be able to focus on—"

I elbowed him to shut him up. Someone was hurrying toward us.

It was Anson, the stressed-out PA. I was surprised to see that he was sporting a pretty impressive shiner.

"Whoa, dude!" I said to him. "What happened? You pick a fight with a pro boxer or something?"

Anson looked nervous. "No, nothing like that," he said. "I wasn't looking where I was going and ran into one of the camera booms."

I couldn't help being skeptical. I've had a few black eyes in my day. You didn't get one like *that* by bumping into a camera.

But Frank and I had enough mysteries on our plate already. Figuring out who was beating up on some random PA? Not worth the brain cells.

Anson handed some papers to Jaan, then rushed away again. But before we could pick up our conversation about the mission, Stan hurried over.

"We can't keep stopping and starting like this," he said to Jaan with a frown. "Time is money, remember?"

"I'm well aware of that, Stan," Jaan replied calmly. "But one cannot hurry art. . . ."

Frank and I drifted away as they kept talking. "Stan's not the only one in a hurry," I said. "We've got to figure this out before Anya quits. With the way things are going, she might not even wait until the Big Apple Awards."

"I hear you." Frank looked grim. "So what's our next move? Should we try searching a few dressing rooms while everyone's busy out here?"

"Let's do it," I said. We'd done enough talking. I was ready for some action.

"Wait." Frank stopped me before I could take off for the set. "We'd better chill until filming starts again."

I saw his point. We hung out chatting with Buzz for a few minutes until Jaan called for attention.

"Let's take it from the top, my children," he said. "Vance, are you ready? Good. Places, everyone."

"Let's go," I whispered.

Frank and I turned away. We were passing near Jaan's chair when we heard the shrill buzz of his cell phone.

I was close enough to see his face when he glanced at the screen. He frowned, looking annoyed.

"Cut!" he called out, interrupting Vance in midsentence. "I'm sorry, dear people. But I'm afraid I must deal with something important. Relax for a moment and bond with your characters—this won't take long."

He hurried away in the direction of the set. "Guess we'd better hold tight until he gets back," Frank murmured.

"Yeah."

We returned to our spot on the sidelines. Vance was striding around, murmuring his lines under his breath. A makeup person stepped forward to touch up Anya's face while Buzz, Zolo, and Harmony watched. The tech guys fiddled with the cameras and booms. Stan shifted his weight and checked his watch every three seconds. The bodyguards glared menacingly at the reporters hanging around nearby. Everyone else just stood around waiting.

And waiting.

Then waiting some more.

"What's taking him so long?" Vance grumbled.

I knew how he felt. Jaan had been gone for more than twenty minutes.

"This is ridiculous." Stan pulled out his phone and punched in a number. He waited, but finally hung up. "No answer," he announced. "Typical!"

Someone laughed. "That's Jaan for you. He only picks up the phone when he feels like it."

A few people chuckled. But almost everyone looked pretty impatient by now.

"Is it just me," I whispered to Frank, "or are you starting to get a funny feeling about this?"

"Let's go check it out," he murmured. Then he cleared his throat. "We'll run to the set and see what's keeping Jaan," he said loudly. "Be right back!"

"Thanks, boys," Stan said. "Tell Jaan to hurry up and get back here."

We jogged to the set. The place was almost deserted aside from the handful of guards watching the gates. The rest of the cast and crew were out at the location.

"Let's check his office first," Frank said.

"Right."

Jaan's office looked pretty quiet from the outside. As soon as my hand touched the door to knock, it swung wide open.

That's when I saw Jaan. He was bound, gagged, and blindfolded in his office chair with a deadly-looking sword placed across his bloody throat!

Bad Blood

I heard Joe gasp.

"What?" I asked.

Rushing to join him in the doorway, I saw Jaan. "Oh man," I said.

Joe was already inside. "He's alive!" he called, yanking off the blindfold.

Jaan's terrified blue eyes stared back at us. He started to move, struggling against his bonds. A little more blood seeped out of his wound as the sword's blade pressed into it.

I started to reach over and remove the gag. Then, seeing that blood, I changed plans.

"Hold still," I told Jaan. "Let's get this out of the way first."

I checked out the sword, not wanting to grab it wrong and risk slicing his throat open. It was tied around the back of the chair with fishing line. If Jaan tried to move his head or sit up, he'd push right into the sharp blade.

"We need to cut this line," I told Joe, carefully wrapping my hand around the sword's hilt.

"Hold it steady." Joe grabbed a pair of scissors off Jaan's desk and stepped forward. "Jaan, don't move, okay?"

I held my breath as he snipped the line. The sword dropped. I caught it and pulled it away from Jaan's throat.

"Whew!" I said, yanking the other side loose and carefully lowering the sword to the desk.

I knew I'd just messed up any fingerprints that might've been on the handle. But we could worry about that later.

Meanwhile Joe was yanking out the gag. "Oh!" Jaan blurted out as soon as he could speak. "Thank you, my boy."

"Easy," I told him as Joe went to work on the cords around his arms and legs. "Try not to move too much until we get someone to look at that cut."

"Don't worry about that," Jaan said. "It's merely a flesh wound. They pricked me once with the tip and then the blade rubbed it a bit until I realized what they'd done."

"They?" Joe straightened up. "They who?"

Jaan leaned forward. That made his sliced-up throat bubble a little.

"Seriously, man," I said. "Let's get some pressure on that at least."

There was a box of tissues on a side table. I grabbed a handful and pressed them to the wound.

"So what happened?" Joe asked. "Who did this to you?"

"Unfortunately, I have no idea." Jaan looked troubled. "I received a text message telling me that a certain extremely important and delicate delivery had finally arrived and was awaiting signature here in my office. As this delivery is quite late, I was understandably eager to see it safely here."

"What kind of delivery?" I asked.

Jaan waved one hand. "That's not important— it was all a ruse. There was no delivery," he said. "When I entered the office, someone stuck a gun in my back."

"Whoa!" Joe said. "Been there, dude. It's never a good time."

Jaan let out a weak chuckle. "Indeed, I have newfound respect for your line of work, my brave young friends," he said. "In any case, a second person stepped forward and—"

"Hold on," I interrupted. "There were two people?"

"At least two, yes," Jaan replied. "At least I think so. I didn't actually *see* anyone, you understand. The blindfold was the first thing that went on. But it felt as if one person kept the gun poking at me while the other tied me up."

"So they shoved you in the chair, tied you up, and tied that sword to you?" Joe asked.

"My own sword, yes." Jaan glanced at the bloody weapon ruefully. "I imagine it hasn't seen this much action since the end of the Qing dynasty." Then he turned back to us. "Oh! And I nearly forgot—before they left, they rubbed something on me, just here. . . ."

He fiddled with his shirt, pulling back the collar. His chest was smeared with what looked like his own blood.

"Whoa!" Joe said when he got a look.

I just stared. The blood spelled out two words: FOR ANYA.

Pulling out my phone, I used it to snap a few photos. "Okay, I think it's safe to say our culprit has struck again," I said.

Jaan had pulled out a small mirror by then and

was peering at the words. "Oh, dear," he said. "I suppose you're right."

Just then Stan burst into the office. "What's going on in here?" he said. When he got a look at Jaan, his jaw dropped, and he let out a curse word or two.

"Relax, Stan," Jaan said. "I'm all right."

"When these two didn't return either, I figured I'd better come myself and see what was going on," Stan exclaimed. "I never expected something like this!" He yanked his phone out of his pocket. "I'm calling an ambulance."

I gulped down half my soda, then set the glass down on the table. "This has got to be the craziest mission yet," I told Joe. We were in a booth in the back of a diner a few blocks from the Empire State Building.

"I hear ya, bro." Joe picked at the sandwich the waitress had just brought him. "I wish we could've questioned Jaan a little more before Stan got there."

"Me too. But we couldn't—not without blowing our cover." I sighed. "They probably won't keep him long at the hospital. We can catch him when he's released."

"And until then?"

I shrugged. "Not much chance of getting any useful info back on set."

That was an understatement. The police had swarmed Jaan's office, checking out the scene of the crime. Filming had been called off for the day, but nobody seemed ready to leave. Actors, crew members, PAs, and more were milling around. Plus, there were more reporters and TV cameras than ever. Anya was huddled in one of the trailers with Harmony, Vivian, and a couple of bodyguards. There was no way we'd be able to search any dressing rooms or sniff around Jaan's office anytime soon.

"I still think we should've clued the cops in as to why we were there," Joe said. "Then they would've shared any info they found."

"We can get the report from ATAC HQ later. We can't blow our cover now."

"Yeah, I know. So all we can do is sit around and talk—as usual." Joe took a bite of his sandwich.

We'd been talking since arriving at the diner. Mostly about how Jaan thought there were two people involved in his attack. Did that mean we'd been chasing a team of bad guys all along?

"Well, it obviously wasn't Vance and Amy," I mused. "We saw Vance on the location set at the time it all happened."

"Along with most of our other suspects," Joe pointed out. "Buzz, Stan, Zolo—they were all right there waiting to film the whole time Jaan was gone. And unless Jaan did this to himself . . ."

"I don't know if he's nutty enough to dream up something like that," I said. "But it would be pretty much physically impossible to set himself up with the sword at his throat and all that."

"Unless *he's* the one with an accomplice," Joe pointed out.

"Still seems far-fetched," I said. "So who does that leave us?"

"Just Big Bobby. Think he could be in cahoots with someone else?"

"It's possible," I said. "That could explain how he got access to the set. He could be working with one of the other bodyguards, a friend from the crew, whoever."

"And the bloody Anya message on Jaan's chest plays right into his motive," Joe added.

"Not really. Why would Big Bobby want to hurt Jaan? Jaan's been Anya's biggest supporter all along."

"Yeah, but he also fired Big Bobby," Joe said. "Maybe the big man's mad because Jaan, like, separated him from his true love or whatever."

I stared into my drink, thinking about that. "I

guess it's possible. But it still doesn't explain the earlier stuff. It makes no sense that he'd threaten Anya before he got fired. Or at all, really, if he claims to love her."

"It's like I said before," Joe said. "Maybe he thought if she was scared, she'd want his protection even more."

That still didn't make much sense to me. But what did I know about how a guy like that might think?

I slid toward the end of the booth. "Let's get out of here," I said. "We should go talk to Anya about Big Bobby again."

Soon we were knocking on the door of Harmony's trailer. Vivian answered the door, looking cautious.

"Oh, it's you," she said when she recognized us. "Come on in—Anya's here."

"Is that Frank and Joe?" Anya rushed to greet us as we stepped inside. "Where have you guys been?"

"Tsk, tsk," Vivian clucked. "You shouldn't leave your girlfriend wondering where you are at such a stressful time, Frank."

"Um, sorry," I mumbled. "We just, uh . . ." I shot a desperate glance toward Joe.

"We came as soon as we could," he said smoothly. "The police wanted to ask us a few questions, since we're the ones who found Jaan."

"See?" Harmony told Vivian. "I told you that was probably it."

"Sorry, young man," Vivian told me, taking a seat beside Harmony on the sofa. "I'm just a bit protective of our Anya, that's all. She has so few true friends around here." She shrugged. "But that's Hollywood for you, I suppose."

I wasn't too interested in discussing the ins and outs of Hollywood. Anya was clinging to my arm, making me nervous. The bodyguards were staring at me. Besides, it wasn't like we could question Anya in front of these people.

"Let's get out of here, okay?" I told her.

Anya glanced nervously at the door. "Are you sure? Aren't there tons of reporters outside?"

"Not that many," Joe lied. "Anyway, we'll just jump in a cab. It'll be fine—you'll feel better once you're away from this place."

"Maybe you're right." Anya looked up at me. "Okay, let's go."

Moose hoisted himself to his feet. "It's okay, dude," Joe told him. "We'll take it from here."

"You sure?" Moose rumbled.

Anya nodded. "It's okay, Moose. Thanks. I'll see you tomorrow."

We headed for the door. "Wait, dear," Vivian called. "You forgot your purse."

"Oops." Anya dropped my arm. "You're right. I'm so freaked out right now, I'd forget my own head if it wasn't attached!"

Soon the three of us were outside. The tabloid reporters started shouting questions at Anya from over behind the barricades. Luckily, the guards were doing a good job holding them back.

"So what was that all about?" Anya asked, turning her back to the reporters. "Why'd you want me to come with you?"

"We need to ask you a few questions," I said.

"About Big Bobby," Joe added. "We're kind of thinking he might've been involved in Jaan's attack."

Anya looked alarmed. "Really? Why?"

We told her. When she heard about the bloody message, she looked uncomfortable and a little sick.

"Oh, wow," she murmured. "Actually, there's something I probably should show you. . . ."

She snapped open her purse and stuck her hand inside. Then she gasped.

"Oh!" she cried.

She let go of the purse. It fell to the ground, leaving her other hand visible.

Along with the ugly four-inch-long yellow scorpion clamped onto one finger.

Getting the Message

"**A**nya!" Frank cried.

There was no answer. She slumped to the ground. Frank barely jumped forward in time to catch her.

"Where'd that thing come from?" I exclaimed.

"I don't know. But get it off her!"

Yeah. How exactly was I supposed to do that?

Luckily, the scorpion took care of that itself. Letting go of Anya's finger, it dropped to the ground and started to skitter off.

"Catch it!" Frank yelled.

No way was I grabbing that thing with my bare hands. I was ready to stomp on it when I spotted Anya's purse lying where she'd dropped it.

I grabbed the purse, then pulled that Deathstalker key chain out of my pocket. "Get in there, you beast!" I muttered, giving the real scorpion a flick with the fake one.

The gross little creature went flying into the purse. I snapped it shut, then glanced over at Anya.

"Is she—you know, dead?" I asked.

Frank looked annoyed. "Don't you ever pay attention in our ATAC seminars?" he asked. "They totally covered this kind of thing in the one about neurotoxins. If that's a deathstalker scorpion—and I'm guessing it is—it's pretty venomous. But a healthy person isn't going to die from its sting as long as he or she gets medical attention."

Just then the trailer door flew open. "What's going on?" Harmony asked. "Did someone scream out here?" Then she spotted Anya and let out a shriek. "What happened?"

The others were already crowded around her in the doorway. A guard or two had come over by now too. There didn't seem much chance of keeping this quiet, so we told everyone what had happened.

"The sting itself wouldn't have knocked her out, I don't think," Frank said. "She probably just fainted out of shock. She'll be fine—as long as we get her to a hospital for some antivenin." He shot me a look.

Okay, I can take a hint. Pulling out my phone, I dialed 911.

"Hey, at least the ambulance should already know the way to the set," I quipped weakly.

"Wow," I said as Anya let us into her hotel suite. "This place doesn't look like our room."

Anya smiled wanly. "It's nice, isn't it?"

Nice? Try amazing.

The main room was about the size of a basketball court. Well, close, anyway. There were plush leather sofas, a seriously awesome entertainment system, and a kitchenette in one corner. Through one door I spied a huge bathroom with a spa tub. Next door was the bedroom, which was almost as big as the main room.

Frank barely glanced around the suite. "Are you sure you're up to talking?" he asked, helping Anya over to the nearest sofa.

"I'm okay. I want to do whatever it takes to figure out who's doing this." She glanced at the bandage on the hand where she'd been stung. "Because I'm starting to think I don't even want to wait until the Big Apple Awards. I'm ready to go home and forget about this whole acting thing right now!"

Uh-oh. She sounded pretty shaken. No wonder. It's not every day you get stung by a venomous scorpion in the middle of New York City.

"So you have no idea how that thing got in your purse?" I said, perching on the arm of the sofa.

She glanced at me and narrowed her eyes. "What do you think?"

"Okay, dumb question." I grinned.

"What were you going to tell us before?" Frank asked her. "That's why you were reaching into your purse, right? You said you had something to show us."

I shot him an admiring look. Dude might be kind of nerdy, but he's got a great memory.

"Oh, right. I almost forgot," Anya said. "I was reaching for my phone. Big Bobby sent me a couple more messages."

"Really?" I sat up straight.

She nodded. "I thought you guys were crazy to worry about him before. But now I'm not so sure. He's getting kind of . . . pushy."

"What do the messages say?" Frank asked.

Anya pulled her phone out of her pocket. Someone at the hospital had removed the scorpion, but she'd told them she didn't want her purse back.

I didn't blame her. That scorpion was creepy.

The film's animal wrangler had turned up to retrieve it and seemed relieved that it hadn't been hurt.

Me? I wouldn't have minded seeing it squished. I love animals, okay? Just not the ones that can kill you.

Anya scrolled through her texts. "Just more of the same. He loves me, he wants another chance to prove it. That kind of thing." She held out the phone so we could scan a couple of the messages. "Anyway, it was starting to freak me out, so I finally sent him a text back."

"Uh-oh," Frank said. "Not sure that was the best idea."

"What'd you say?" I asked.

"I asked him about all the weird, scary stuff that's been happening on set. Whether he knew anything about it."

"Did he respond?" Frank asked.

"Yeah." Anya held out the phone again so we could read the latest message:

SORRY 2 HEAR UR SCARED. THE CAMERA ALMOST FALLING ON U WAS TERRIBLE. SO WAS THE MESSED-UP WIND TUNNEL. THOSE THINGS SHOULD NEVER HAVE HAPPENED. BUT DON'T WORRY, I TOOK CARE OF IT. THE ONES RESPONSIBLE NOW KNOW BETTER THAN 2 LET ANYTHING LIKE THAT HAPPEN

AGAIN. I ONLY WANT 2 PROTECT U—I'M ALWAYS ON UR SIDE. LOVE 4EVR, BB

"Whoa. He sounds pretty intense," I said. "So you asked him about the camera thing and Barb's accident?"

"Actually, no," said Anya. "I didn't really go into specifics. I just said I was scared."

"Hmm." Frank scanned the text again. "So does this mean Big Bobby really didn't have anything to do with those accidents? Or is he just trying to cover his tracks?"

"Good question," I said. "And what do you think he means when he says he 'took care of it'? Could he be referring to Jaan's attack earlier?"

"You think Big Bobby did that?" Anya looked alarmed. "But how? He's not allowed on set!"

"We know," I said. "We're thinking he has an accomplice. Maybe one of the other bodyguards, or somebody else he's friends with from the crew."

"Besides, it would've been a little easier to sneak in this morning when everyone was prepping for the scene," Frank said. Just then the phone buzzed in his hand. "Incoming," he added, handing it back to Anya.

She took it and scanned the new message. "It's from Big Bobby!" she exclaimed.

"No way!" I said. "Let's see it."

This time the text was brief:

JUST HEARD U GOT STUNG. 2 MAD 2 C STR8 RIGHT NOW. BUT DON'T WORRY, MY LOVE—I WILL FIND OUT WHO DID THIS TO U. AND I WILL MAKE THEM PAY.

Following the Trail

"I'm still not sure we should've left her alone up there." Joe glanced up at the tall brick facade of the hotel.

"You never want to leave a pretty girl alone anywhere," I quipped, though my heart wasn't really in it.

I wasn't sure we should have left Anya either. She was pretty freaked out. At least we'd convinced her to give us a little more time to figure out what was going on. She'd agreed to stick to her old deadline. We had until the Big Apple Awards—just days away now.

"The best thing for her right now is to get some sleep," I said. "But not us. We need to figure out this case."

"No kidding. Starting with where the heck that scorpion came from and how it got in Anya's purse."

"Jaan can tell us if a live scorpion is being used on the movie," I said. "I'll try calling him to find out for sure."

I called Jaan's cell. No answer.

"Let's head back to the set," Joe suggested as I hung up. "Maybe he's there."

It was about six p.m. by then, and the streets were crazy. There was no way we were getting a cab. So we started walking.

"Big Bobby's last text seemed to be about the scorpion thing," I said. "Which means he didn't do it."

"But he's mad at whoever did," Joe finished. "Kind of like he claimed to be mad at whoever knocked over that camera and messed with the wind tunnel."

"Think he's telling the truth about that?" I said. "If so, it looks like we're definitely dealing with more than one person who is causing trouble."

"Right there with you, bro." Joe dodged a couple of commuters rushing for a bus. "So we have one culprit targeting Anya, then another one—Big Bobby—playing vigilante and trying to keep her safe. And he appears to be working with an accomplice, if Jaan was right about two people having attacked him."

I frowned. "Yes, and speaking of Jaan," I said, "if he's the one who's going after Anya, maybe that's the real reason he fired Big Bobby."

"Makes sense, I guess." Joe stopped at a red light and glanced at me. "And now Big Bobby's going after him. Trying to keep Anya safe."

"But what if it's *not* Jaan?" I said. "What if Big Bobby just *thinks* it was him who rigged that camera and the wind tunnel and the rest?"

"Big Bobby could be punishing the wrong guy." Joe pulled out his cell phone as the light changed. "Either way, we probably need to warn Jaan. If Big Bobby was the one who pulled that sword stunt, he's obviously kind of unbalanced."

Once again, there was no answer on Jaan's phone. "Try calling the hospital," I suggested. "Maybe they didn't release him yet."

Joe nodded and started to dial. He spoke to whoever answered, and then hung up.

"He's not there," he reported. "The receptionist said he checked himself out exactly fifteen minutes ago."

"For real?" I stopped in the middle of the sidewalk and stared at him. A passing New Yorker cursed at me for blocking his way, but I barely heard it. "You know what this means, right?"

"That Jaan doesn't like hospitals?"

"No, it means there's no way he could've planted that scorpion," I said. "He was in the hospital at the time it happened. At least according to what Anya told us about when her purse could have been unattended for someone to put the scorpion in there."

"So he's not our guy?"

"Not unless he has an accomplice." I sighed. "Man, this is getting way too complicated! It seems like there's no one who could've done all this stuff. No one with the right combo of access, motive, and timing."

"What about Stan?" Joe said.

"What about him? You think he could be working with Jaan?"

"Doubtful. Those two don't seem like best buds." Joe started walking again. I fell into step beside him. "But what if Jaan's not involved at all? What if Stan's been doing the stuff, but Big Bobby *thinks* it was Jaan, so that's who he's going after?"

I grabbed my phone. "Whatever else we do, we'd better let ATAC know our suspicions about Big Bobby," I said, texting as I talked. "Might be worth having them bring him in for questioning. Just in case."

"Yeah. In the meantime, let's get a move on. Jaan could be in serious danger and not even know it."

We rushed the rest of the way to the set. It was pretty much closing down for the evening. The only people still around were a few members of the catering staff, a random PA or two, some bodyguards and crew people, and the props master.

"Jaan?" the props master said when we asked her. "Haven't seen him since they carted him off to the hospital."

"What about Stan?" I asked her.

"He left almost an hour ago," she said. "The actors are all long gone too."

"So you're in charge of all the stuff that appears in the film, right?" Joe asked.

She cocked an eyebrow, looking a little startled by the abrupt change of topic. "That's right," she said. "Um, aren't you an extra? Is this your first job or something?"

"Yeah, he's new to all this," I answered quickly. I'd already guessed where Joe was going with his question. "So are you in charge of, you know, animals, too?"

"Sort of," she said. "There's an animal wrangler

who does the day-to-day, but it's all part of my job, yes."

"So do you know anything about the scorpion?" Joe asked. "The one that stung Anya?"

She grimaced. "We were supposed to get that shipment three days ago. Someone called the wrangler this morning to let him know it was finally coming."

Maybe this was the important delivery that Jaan had been waiting for.

"So the animal wrangler picked up the package?" I asked.

"He was supposed to." The woman looked annoyed, though I was pretty sure it wasn't aimed at us. "He got called away at the last minute. Someone else had to run over and pick it up instead."

"Really? Who?" Joe looked interested.

"No clue. Probably one of the PAs." The props master checked her watch. "Anyway, it's all handled now. The scorpion is here safe and sound, and from what I hear, Anya's going to be fine. Now if you'll excuse me . . ."

She hurried off. I stared at Joe. "I wonder which PA picked up that package?" I said slowly.

"What's the diff?"

"I'm thinking about a certain PA, and a certain incident with a certain box of explosives," I said.

"What if Jaan really was the one who told Anson to have us move those boxes?"

Joe shrugged. "So? We already asked Anson, and he claimed he didn't remember who gave him the order."

"But that's just it. What if Anson wasn't an innocent pawn after all? What if he's been Jaan's accomplice all along?"

Joe raised an eyebrow. "Interesting theory. As a PA, he has full access to the set. Nobody thinks twice about seeing him around."

I nodded. "If he's been working with Jaan, maybe he picked up that scorpion—and then planted it in Anya's purse. He probably has keys to all the trailers, right?"

"Or knows where to get them." Joe looked thoughtful. "But wait—was he at the convention?"

We thought about it, but neither of us could remember. "The guy just blends into the background," I said with a sigh of frustration.

"Yeah. Makes him the perfect accomplice," Joe agreed. "In fact, are we sure it's Jaan he's working with? Could just as easily be Stan."

"Or Buzz," I agreed. "Or even Vance. Any of those guys probably could've pulled off the stuff that happened at the con even if Anson wasn't there to help."

Joe nodded. "I'm thinking it's time to have a little talk with Anson."

"Ditto."

We searched the set. Even more people had left by now, but one of the guards pointed us to the costume tent. We found Anson in there sorting through some paperwork.

"Hey," Joe greeted him, keeping his voice casual. "So we heard you were the person who picked up the scorpion delivery today."

"What?" Anson straightened up and spun around. "Oh my gosh! Are you serious? The scorpion finally got here?"

I blinked and glanced at Joe, confused. "Uh, yeah," I told Anson. "Like Joe said, we heard you picked up the package."

"Wasn't me," Anson said. "But wow, what a relief! Fred was starting to worry it got lost in transit. He must be super relieved."

"Probably, I guess." I watched him carefully. "I guess you heard the scorpion ended up stinging Anya, right?"

"What?" Anson's wide eyes opened even wider. "Oh my gosh, those things are super venomous! Is she okay?"

"She'll be fine," I said. "No thanks to whoever put that scorpion in her purse."

"Who did that?" Anson sounded kind of agitated now. "Who would even do something like that? That's horrible!"

"That's what we're wondering," I said. "Look, are you sure you—"

"Wow, look at the time!" Joe interrupted loudly. "Come on, Frank. We're going to be late."

"Huh?" I said as he grabbed my arm and dragged me out of the costume tent. "What are you doing?" I hissed. "I just had him going!"

"I know. But we've had enough talking." Joe pulled me behind a stack of sound equipment. "It's time for some good old-fashioned secret agent work. If Anson's involved, he must realize we're onto him now. So let's hide here until he comes out, then follow him."

I frowned, a little skeptical of the plan. It sounded like something that would work better in a movie than in real life.

"We don't have time to indulge your ADHD action hero fantasies right now," I said. "We'd be better off working on him some more, trying to get him to say something incriminating."

"Just humor me, okay? If this doesn't work— *shhh!*" Suddenly Joe ducked lower. "Here he comes."

I peeked out. Anson had just emerged from the

costume tent. After glancing around carefully, he hurried toward the gate.

"Let's go!" Joe urged, bounding out and tiptoeing after him.

I sighed and followed. What choice did I have?

"This is crazy," I whispered. "We're wasting time we don't have. We should be tracking down Jaan, or talking to Stan, or—"

"Hurry! He's getting away." Joe put on a burst of speed as Anson disappeared through the gate.

After leaving the set, he crisscrossed through the city for a few blocks. We stayed about half a block behind him, hidden by the crowds of evening commuters.

"He's probably just heading back to the hotel," I told Joe quietly.

Joe yanked me into a doorway as Anson paused at a corner and glanced back over his shoulder. "The hotel is in the other direction, dude," he whispered.

"Okay, so he's in search of decent Thai food," I said as we hurried to the corner. "I still don't think this—"

I stopped short as we rounded the corner. Anson was just a few yards ahead, talking to someone. Someone big. With bright red hair.

"Big Bobby!" Joe blurted out.

A Need for Speed

First rule of undercover tracking? Don't yell out your suspect's name while you're tracking him.

Oops.

Big Bobby and Anson spun around and spotted us. Anson seemed like he wanted to take off but hesitated.

Big Bobby didn't look quite as panicked. He glared at us for a second, as if he was deciding if he could take us both on at once.

For the record? I'm thinking he could have.

But he didn't. Looking around at all the random bystanders on the block, he took a few quick steps forward and grabbed Anson with one meaty paw. They dashed to the curb, where a balding businessman had just hailed a cab.

"Sorry, man," he growled in an intimidating voice. "We need this worse than you do."

Then he flung Anson into the back of the cab and jumped in himself.

"Hey!" the businessman yelled as the taxi peeled away from the block. "That's my cab!"

I was already at the curb, waving my hand wildly. By some miracle, a free cab was just passing by. It zipped over to me, cutting off five or six other vehicles.

"Hurry!" I yelled to Frank over the blare of car horns. "Get in!"

Ignoring the businessman's dirty look, I jumped into the cab. The driver glanced back at us. He was a sweaty guy with a serious five o'clock shadow and eyebrows so bushy he looked like a Muppet.

"Where'll it be, boys?" he asked in a thick Brooklyn accent.

"Follow that cab!" I pointed at the other taxi, which was already speeding across the next intersection. Then I grinned and looked at Frank, who'd just flopped onto the patched vinyl seat beside me. "I've kind of always wanted to say that."

The driver steered out into traffic, ignoring another round of honking horns as he followed the other taxi. "They friends of yours?" he asked.

"Not exactly," I replied. "More like some acquaintances who are up to no good."

The guy shot me a suspicious look in the rearview mirror. "You for real?" he asked. "This ain't one of them college pranks or something, is it?"

He was already slowing down. Uh-oh. We had to do something—fast. Another few seconds and that other cab would disappear into the crazy Manhattan traffic.

Desperate times called for desperate measures. "Look, we're totally serious, uh"—I leaned forward to get a look at the name badge on the dashboard—"Demetri. If you catch that other cab, there's a big tip in it for you."

I pulled out my wallet and yanked out the bill hidden behind my fake driver's license: my own private Benjamin. It was the hundred-dollar bill that ATAC gave us in case of emergencies.

All it took was one glance at the C-note. "You're the boss," Demetri said, stepping on the gas. "Hold on!"

"And don't worry about getting a ticket," I added. "If you do, we'll pay it."

Frank looked alarmed as the taxi gained speed. "Whoa!" he exclaimed as our cab narrowly missed sideswiping a city bus.

Demetri glanced back again, looking amused.

"Your friend here scares easy, huh?" he asked me.

I grinned. "Pretty much."

Frank looked annoyed. "Can we keep our eyes on the road, maybe?"

Demetri shrugged. "Whatever. Hold on, boys—looks like we're turning."

The other taxi was skidding around the corner up ahead. We followed, dodging a couple of slow-paced SUVs as we made the turn onto Seventh Avenue.

"They're heading downtown," Frank said, clinging to the door handle to keep from sliding around as Demetri weaved in and out of traffic.

I leaned forward for a better look. "I see Anson peeking out the back window. I think they're onto us."

A second later the cab ahead took another sharp turn, disappearing down a side street. Demetri had to stomp the brake so hard that the tires screamed in protest.

"Yeah," Frank said, hanging on. "I'd say they're definitely onto us."

An old lady walking a poodle had to jump back as we barely made the turn onto the side street. West 24th, I think. It was hard to tell for sure. The sign went by pretty fast.

Demetri was grinning as he spun the wheel to

straighten out, then hit the gas again. "Yo, this is kind of fun."

He was right. It kind of was. The cabs flew up one street and down the next, zipping through red lights, narrowly avoiding sideswiping parked cars, rounding corners at breakneck speed, scattering pedestrians left and right.

All the while, the other cab stayed maybe half a block ahead. Apparently their driver was just as nuts as Demetri. Even the narrow, mazelike streets of the West Village didn't slow him down much.

Somehow neither cab actually ran anyone over. But drivers sure honked at us. And cursed at us. As we raced through the NYU campus, a few groups of students even hooted and cheered us on.

"This is crazy." Frank's teeth were gritted. I guess he wasn't having as much fun as I was. "Someone's going to get killed. Possibly us."

"Don't worry. Demetri will take care of us," I assured him.

"You got that right, buddy." Demetri spun the wheel, following the other driver as he skidded around the corner onto Park Avenue.

"Back uptown," I commented.

"Seriously," Frank said. "What are we hoping to accomplish now? We pretty much know those two are working together at this point. All we have to do is tell the authorities, and case closed."

"Not if the two of them disappear tonight," I said. "Anyway, don't worry. Manhattan is an island, remember? They can't get away without crossing a bridge or tunnel."

Demetri snorted loudly. "Yeah, good luck with that this time of day," he said. "You could catch 'em on foot if they got stuck in one of those lines!"

"See?" I smiled at Frank. "They're totally ours. Nothing can stop us."

The whine of a siren cut off his response. "Uh-oh." Demetri glanced in the rearview mirror. "Cops."

The other cab had heard the siren too. "Hey, they're pulling over!" Frank said.

"Stop!" I exclaimed.

Big Bobby and Anson were jumping out of their cab before ours made it to the curb. I tossed the hundred-dollar bill onto the front seat, along with a card with our real contact info.

"Send us the bill for the ticket, Demetri," I said as I flung open the door. "And thanks!"

"Yo, you better let me know how it turns out!" The cabbie's voice floated after us as we leaped out of the cab.

I tossed him a thumbs-up. "You got it, dude!"

"That way!" Frank pointed.

Big Bobby and Anson were sprinting up the sidewalk.

"Hurry!" I exclaimed. "We can't let them out of our sight."

I was feeling pretty good as we took off. Frank and I are both fast runners. The pair we were chasing? Not so much—or so I guessed. Big Bobby was way more of a battleship than a speedboat. And Anson looked like the kid who always got picked last in gym class.

"We've got them now," I panted as we sprinted across the intersection at East 41st Street.

"They're almost to Forty-second," Frank replied, focused on the runners ahead. "They'll have to turn there—Park Avenue dead-ends at Grand Central."

We put on a burst of speed.

As we reached the corner, I saw the pair racing across the broad, busy expanse of 42nd Street. The light had just blinked to green, and car horns blared.

"Oh man!" I skidded to a stop, standing on tiptoe to peer over the steady line of taxis, cars, trucks, and buses pouring past. "We've got to get across before they get away!"

Frank looked at me. "You scare easy, huh?" he

quipped. Then he stepped off the curb, holding up both hands.

I winced as a delivery truck barreled toward him. I was pretty sure I was about to see my brother crushed into a pulp right there on 42nd Street.

But the truck screeched to a halt just in time, causing the driver to lay on his horn. He leaned out the window.

"What, are you some kind of moron?" he shouted at Frank.

But Frank was already moving on, jogging right in front of several lanes of traffic, forcing the cars to stop or run him over. Lucky for him, the drivers all chose option number one.

Kids? Don't try this at home. Especially if home happens to be midtown Manhattan.

But we survived. Seconds later we were both on the north side of the street.

"There!" I pointed, spotting Big Bobby's red hair bobbing above the rest of the pedestrians. "They're going into the train station!"

Grand Central Terminal was pretty crowded. Luckily, Big Bobby is an easy guy to pick out of a crowd. We spotted him near the information booth in the center of the main concourse. Anson was right on his heels.

They were still moving pretty fast, shoving

commuters out of their way at every step. Well, Big Bobby was, anyway. Anson was just sort of following in his wake.

"Looks like they're heading for the stairs," Frank said. "They probably hope we won't think to look for them on the lower level."

"Let's go."

We reached the stairs just seconds after they disappeared down them. Taking the steps three at a time, we skidded to a stop at the bottom.

"Now what?" I said.

Frank peered up and down the sloping hallway. There were fewer people down here. That made it easy to see that Big Bobby and Anson were nowhere in sight.

"Maybe they went in there." Frank pointed to the arched entrance to the Oyster Bar, the famous old seafood restaurant. Mom and Dad and Frank and I had met Aunt Trudy there a few times when we were little kids. She'd still lived in the city then.

"Let's find out," I said, heading for the entrance.

The Oyster Bar was divided into two sections. To the left, there was a fancier sit-down area. To the right, a cavernous open space was filled with a bunch of old-school lunch counters. People were seated on the little stools over there, sucking down raw oysters and clams.

Except for two people: Big Bobby and Anson. They were vaulting over the bar at the back of the room, landing in the oyster shucking area.

"Hey!" one of the shuckers exclaimed. "You aren't allowed back here!"

We broke into a run, almost crashing into a waitress carrying a tray of oysters. She was probably in her sixties. Her hair was glossy platinum blond, and her bright makeup would've looked right at home on the movie set.

"Sorry, ma'am," Frank said breathlessly, reaching out a hand to steady her tray as he dashed past. "Really sorry."

"Wait!" she snapped. "Young man . . ."

I didn't hear the rest. Big Bobby had just stopped behind the counter. He turned to face us. Anson stopped too, cowering behind him.

Frank and I skidded to a halt on our side of the counter. For a second we all just stared at one another. The oyster shuckers and the waitress were yelling, but we didn't pay any attention.

Big Bobby was, well, *big*. Really big.

If he wanted to, he could just reach out, knock our heads together, and leave us lying there. He could be gone before we even woke up or the cops arrived.

And I was pretty sure he'd just realized that too.

A slow grin spread across his face. "Well, you caught me," he said. "Anya would be super impressed, I'm sure. What are you gonna do to me now, lover boy?"

He smirked at Frank. Frank gulped and shot me a sidelong look. I knew what he was thinking, because I was thinking the same thing.

We'd caught up to the bad guys.

Now what?

A Final Surprise

"Hold it right there, sonny!" As Joe and I stood frozen like statues, the bottle-blond waitress pushed past us. She marched up to the counter and glared at Big Bobby and Anson. "Just what do you think you're doing?"

Big Bobby blinked, looking confused. "Huh?"

She shook a finger in his face. "I just told Marge to call the police," she said. "This is an eating establishment, not a gym!"

Big Bobby frowned. "This is none of your business, lady," he snapped. "Now step aside—I need to teach these two losers a lesson."

"Not so fast." The waitress didn't budge. "Stay where you are if you know what's good for you."

Big Bobby looked incredulous. He started to laugh, then snorted. "Outta the way, you old bag."

He started to push his way out through the little entrance in the counter. But the waitress stepped over to block his way.

"Maybe you didn't hear me," she said. "I told you to stop."

"Who's gonna make me?" Big Bobby scoffed.

I looked at Joe. We had to do something—we couldn't let innocent bystanders get caught up in the middle of this.

"Listen," I began. "Let's all just calm down and—"

Before I could finish, the waitress grabbed a squirt bottle off the counter.

SPLURT! She aimed it right into Big Bobby's face.

"Ow, my eyes!" Big Bobby shouted, grabbing his face. "Ow-ow-ow!"

"What was that?" Anson exclaimed, sounding panicky. Even more panicky than usual, that is.

The waitress smirked. "Hot sauce," she said. "Best in the city. Want a taste?"

She aimed the bottle at Anson. He backed up. "Um, no thanks, ma'am."

His eyes were darting around. He was clearly looking for an escape route.

"Watch him," I warned Joe.

"You going somewhere, fella?" One of the oyster shuckers stepped forward, soon joined by a couple of his friends. They were all wielding the sharp little knives they used to detach the oysters from their shells. "Because I'm thinking maybe you'd better stick around till we get this sorted out."

Anson let out a squeak of terror. Joe grinned and gave the waitress an admiring look. She was still standing in front of Big Bobby, squirt bottle at the ready.

"That's what I like," Joe said. "A woman who doesn't scare easily."

"What an exciting chase," Jaan said, picking at the bandage on his throat. "Sounds like a scene I'd love to shoot."

Joe and I were in his hotel suite, which was just as luxurious as Anya's right down the hall. We'd just finished filling him in on what had happened. The waitress and the oyster shuckers had kept Big Bobby and Anson at bay until the police arrived. Joe and I had passed the time questioning the pair. Once he realized he was busted, Big Bobby had confessed to a lot of the recent trouble. He claimed he'd done it all out of love for Anya.

As for Anson? He didn't care much about Anya one way or the other. Apparently, Anson had messed up some permit paperwork, which caused delays in shooting and cost the production a lot of money. No one knew who was to blame, but Big Bobby found out and threatened to tell Stan and get Anson fired if he didn't help him.

"I suppose it's not that much of a surprise that Bobby was our culprit," Jaan said, shaking his head sadly. "At least not after what I found out earlier today."

"What did you find out?" Joe asked.

Jaan sighed, sinking back into the soft cushions of his chair. "I heard from one of my colleagues— one of those who recommended Big Bobby to me. It seems he did so mostly to get him out of his own hair. Apparently Bobby was pestering one of the actresses on his set too."

"Really?" I said. "So this has happened before?"

"Not to such an extent, perhaps," Jaan replied. "But I made a few more calls after that, and yes, it appears our Bobby has a habit of being a bit too emotionally invested in his work."

"Wow," Joe said. "Too bad nobody clued you in sooner. Might've saved us all a lot of trouble."

"And poor Barb her life." Jaan looked sad. "I suppose that one will haunt all of us—especially

Big Bobby. He may be confused, but I'm quite convinced he's not a monster."

I frowned. "Actually, he didn't confess to messing with that wind tunnel netting."

That had been bugging me ever since the cops had dragged off the pair. Once Big Bobby started talking, he'd confessed willingly to the attack on Jaan, the fire at the convention, and even trying to blow me up with that box of explosives.

He'd actually apologized for that last one. He said he'd gone a little crazy with jealousy when he'd heard Anya had a boyfriend.

Yeah. A little crazy, all right . . .

Then, when we asked him about the wind tunnel? His whole expression had changed.

"I'd never do anything that might hurt Anya!" he'd fumed angrily. He'd looked so outraged that the oyster shuckers had to back him off with their knives.

"So if you didn't do it, who did?" I'd asked him. "And what about the other stuff that hurt Anya, or could have? The falling camera, the scorpion . . ."

"The falling camera was him." Big Bobby had turned to glare at Anson. "I only told him to scare her a little—you know, remind her that she was a lot safer when I was around. But he took it too far. *Way* too far." Anson swallowed hard and backed away a few steps.

So that explained Anson's shiner and the text Big Bobby had sent to Anya saying he'd taken care of things.

"Yeah, it's weird," Joe said to Jaan, snapping me back to the here and now. "He wouldn't fess up to the electrified microphone at the convention, either . . . or the original dressing room fire . . . or those unidentified text threats from before . . . or the cut-up photo Anya found in her trailer."

I nodded. "We thought most of that stuff was part of his plan to scare Anya into needing him to protect her," I put in. "But he claims he didn't even know about the texts, and that he had nothing to do with the other incidents."

Jaan looked puzzled. "That is a bit odd," he said. "Let's call the police and see what they've found out so far, hmm?"

He placed the call, putting it on speakerphone. The officer who answered sounded kind of distracted. He took down Jaan's info, promising that someone would call him back as soon as Big Bobby and Anson had finished their interviews and processing.

"Ah, well." Jaan shrugged. "I suppose that's all we can do for now, hmm? I'm sure the police will wrangle a full confession from those two."

"Yeah." I chewed my lower lip, still feeling

uneasy. "Isn't that what we said last time we thought we'd solved this thing?"

"Chill out, bro," Joe said, stifling a yawn. "It's been a long day. Let the cops handle it."

We got up to leave. When Jaan swung the door open, someone was standing right outside. It was Zolo. His hand was raised, about to knock.

"Jaan," he said, flicking his eerie green eyes right past Joe and me. "Good, you're still up. Have you seen Anya?"

"Not in quite a while." Jaan raised one bushy gray eyebrow. "She told Vivian she went to bed early, so I didn't expect her at dinner. Why do you ask, my boy?"

"We made plans to do some yoga before bedtime," Zolo said. "You know, to help her relax and get to sleep. But when I just stopped by her room, she didn't answer the door." Finally seeming to register who I was, he turned to me. "You seen her, Boyfriend Frank?"

I shook my head. "Not recently. Joe and I were—um, out for a while."

I wasn't too worried. At least not about Anya. The last time we'd seen her, she'd been exhausted and freaked out. She'd probably just hit the sack early, forgotten about her plans with Zolo, and slept through his knock.

Besides, we'd just caught the bad guys. Hadn't we?

"Oh, dear," Jaan said. "She's probably just deep in dreamland, hmm? But I suppose it wouldn't hurt to check on her—just to be sure."

We all trooped down the plush carpeted hotel hallway. Jaan rapped sharply on Anya's door. Once, twice, a third time.

"Hmm," he said. "Perhaps we should contact hotel security to let us in."

Joe stepped forward and reached for the door handle. "Don't have to," he said. "It's open."

He pushed on the door. It swung open, revealing Anya's darkened suite.

Jaan stepped in and peered into the bedroom. "She's not in there," he said, sounding surprised.

"Looks like the bed hasn't been touched," Zolo added, joining him in the doorway.

I was already checking the bathroom and the kitchen nook. "She's not anywhere in the suite," I reported.

"Don't panic," Joe put in. "Vivian said she skipped dinner, right? Maybe she got hungry and went out to grab a bite."

"Without her wallet? Or her cell phone?" I'd just noticed that both were lying on the coffee table.

Jaan pulled out his own phone. "I'll call the front desk," he said, "to see if she left the building."

Before he could dial, the phone rang. It was the police.

"What'd they say?" I asked when he hung up a few minutes later.

Somehow, I already knew what the answer was going to be before he told us. The cops had questioned Big Bobby and Anson thoroughly. They'd confessed to the same stuff all over again.

But they still insisted they'd had nothing to do with the fire, the texted threats, the electrified mic, or the wind tunnel vandalism.

And now, on top of that, Anya had disappeared without a trace.

"You know what this means, right?" I said to Joe.

He shot me a weary, worried look. "Yeah," he said. "Looks like this mission's not over yet."

FRANKLIN W. DIXON
THE HARDY BOYS

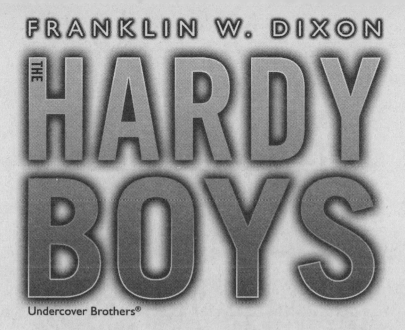

Undercover Brothers®

**INVESTIGATE THESE TWO ADVENTUROUS MYSTERY TRILOGIES
WITH AGENTS FRANK AND JOE HARDY!**

#28 Galaxy X

#29 X-plosion

#30 The X-Factor

#31 Killer Mission

#32 Private Killer

#33 Killer Connections

From Aladdin
Published by Simon & Schuster

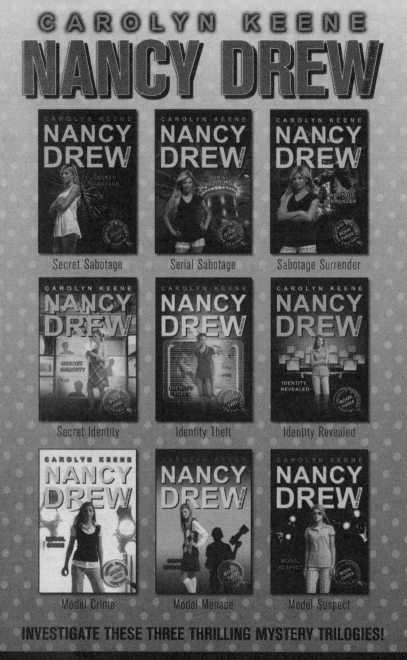

CAROLYN KEENE
NANCY DREW

Secret Sabotage

Serial Sabotage

Sabotage Surrender

Secret Identity

Identity Theft

Identity Revealed

Model Crime

Model Menace

Model Suspect

INVESTIGATE THESE THREE THRILLING MYSTERY TRILOGIES!

CURL UP WITH A GOOD MYSTERY!

From Aladdin
Published by Simon & Schuster